The Fire Opal Mechanism

ALSO BY FRAN WILDE

Updraft
Cloudbound
Horizon
The Jewel and Her Lapidary

THE
FIRE OPAL
MECHANISM

FRAN WILDE

A TOM DOHERTY ASSOCIATES BOOK
NEW YORK

THE FIRE OPAL MECHANISM

Cover illustration by Tommy Arnold
Cover design by Christine Foltzer

Edited by Patrick Nielsen Hayden

A Tor.com Book
Published by Tom Doherty Associates
175 Fifth Avenue
New York, NY 10010

www.tor.com

Tor® is a registered trademark of
Macmillan Publishing Group, LLC.

ISBN 978-1-250-19653-8 (ebook)
ISBN 978-1-250-19654-5 (trade paperback)

First Edition: June 2019

For Beth, and all my favorite librarians

The Fire Opal Mechanism

Among those questioned following the recent unrest—including several Pressmen, professors, and former students—the three-member commission found the testimony of librarian Ania Dem, lately of Far Reaches University, and her companion, the known thief Jorit Lee, by far the most confounding. The following excerpts are accurate examples of the transcript.

Commission Chair Andol: Are you certain you understand the question?

Librarian Dem: While I understand that you wish to make a cohesive history, sirs, I won't let you erase what does not fit. Not this time. The clock forgets nothing. Even if people are often less precise.

The three members of the commission do not react to these truculent words.

Commissioner Andol: But are you certain you remember everything correctly? Where is your proof?

Librarian Ania Dem tucks a few stray graying hairs into the braid coiled around her head. She sips her water, swallows, and adjusts her dark glasses.

Librarian Dem: Yes, we are certain this is the order of the past fortnight's events. Of course we have evidence. We will give it to you once you tell us the Master Archivist is safe.

Several commission members (speaking at once): You are the Master Archivist, madam. There is none other. We suspect you've created an illusory figment in order to evade blame. If another Master Archivist exists, tell us where. And while you're at it, locate the six missing Pressmen as well.

The librarian's mouth purses, as if she is mildly concerned. The commission's questions have grown repetitive.

Librarian Dem: I cannot tell you the Master Archivist's whereabouts, but she does exist. Or did. Her name was Sonoria Vos. I don't know the names of the six Pressmen still missing, nor their whereabouts, either. That was not our fault.

Her hands shake.

Unbidden, the thief speaks: I tell you, Sonoria Vos did exist. Does.

Commissioner Andol (ignoring the outburst): You say you followed another Master Archivist into the past, witnessed moments of the Five Kingdoms that are nowhere in the histories, nor taught in any university. How could you possibly know what you were seeing?

Librarian Dem: I have long experience with the Kingdoms' different eras. I know what I saw.

Commissioner Andol: Of course, but how can you claim to have traveled in time? Where is your proof?

The librarian puts down her water glass. She looks up at the table of commissioners, a tear glimmering behind her glasses.

Librarian Dem: All librarians travel in time, Commissioner. Some more thoroughly than others.

Commissioner's note: Librarian Dem, lately of Far Reaches University, is absolutely dissembling. She and her companions are guilty of something. Given their guilt, it is a matter of debate whether their testimony should be included in the final record.

1.

Ania

As the library's enormous clock ticked past four in the morning, Ania Dem paced its shadowed numbers across the cold slate floor, hurriedly sorting books.

Two worn, hand-bound travel guides from Quadril and the Sindarian Peninsula? Beautifully written. *Hide these.*

The Maniacan Journals about fishing? Boring as sand. *These can be decoys.*

In the deep of night, without students' loud hush all around her, the clock's hour hand ground audibly forward. The clock's gears needed oil, but maintenance would have to wait. In a few hours' time, Ania would cart the decoy books across the university square and bid them good-bye.

The Pressmen gathered at Far Reaches University's gates had demanded the university's books repeatedly.

"The information will not be lost! It will be repurposed, becoming part of the *Universal Compendiums of Knowledge*, for sharing with all, equally," Dean Andol, who had finally conceded, had reassured his staff the afternoon before. "This will buy us more time," he'd added, almost pleading with the teachers assembled in the university square.

Now Ania's usually neat, parchment-colored librarian's robes creased behind her knees. Sweat darkened seams and pleats, but she didn't stop gathering books. She ventured back to the stacks and returned, arms laden with more old texts.

The Collected Biographies of Far Reaches University Presidents: The First Hundred Years? Decoy.

"In the Master Archivist's absence, you must bring books of good number and quality," Dean Andol had added, handing Ania a stack of flyers without meeting her eyes. He'd pointed to carts waiting at the edge of the square. "When we indicate goodwill toward the Pressmen, then perhaps they'll let us finish the term, for the students' sakes."

She'd taken the flyers. Locked the library doors. And then she'd gone to work.

The Book of Gems: A Catalog of the Jeweled Valley Treasury? Had the ancient gems, rumored to whisper secrets and shift reality, ever existed? This one glittering, tooled-leather book hinted they might have. *Keep.*

Ania reached for a brown leather knapsack—the property of the library's Master Archivist—and tucked the gem catalog and the travel guides beneath a shawl.

Dictionaries from across the Six Kingdoms? *To sacrifice?*

All those words. The thought of Pressmen taking those words from her hands, churning them into pulp and ink, and thus into a full set of constantly current *Universal Compendiums of Knowledge* filled Ania's stomach with dread. She'd loved books since she was a child playing in her father's study while he taught his classes. Loved how each volume felt different in the hand, heavy or light; that each smelled of a different era, different knowledge; that they had to be handled carefully—like people—but that they were constant, finished—unlike people. How could she give any of them up?

"But the *Compendiums* could contain everything!" Dean Andol had, the year before, chided the reluctant Master Archivist, Sonoria Vos.

"How does a printing press lay down ink on a page that can twist and rework itself into new forms?" Vos had argued. "And what value do words have across a gap of time if they don't stay put? Books are measures of time. They are made to grow old, to grow, occasionally, wrong."

Ania, listening from the stacks, agreed with her mentor. She liked that books had conversations among themselves. That they, like people, sometimes faded or fell apart when not well cared for. That made them precious.

"The Far Reaches library will not shelve a copy of the *Universal Compendiums* until I can examine the printing process. There's more to any one book, not to mention all of them together, than any 'compendium' can offer. And the conversations between books are equally important. No book can contain everything, Dean Andol."

The dean had left in a huff, and the library had persevered, at least then. Master Archivist Vos—who'd hired Ania long ago—whispered to her as the man's shadow passed beneath the library's great clock. "Books are most valued when they are curated and sought out. When one reference leads to another. I don't trust the Pressmen's approach. Not even if they threaten the gates of the Six Kingdoms' last university."

Now Far Reaches was the only school of its size still standing. The *Compendiums* were everywhere. And Sonoria Vos was nowhere to be found.

Ania grumbled as her braid slipped from its neat coil and draped heavy over her shoulder. Universities across the kingdoms had fallen quieter over the years: fewer scholarly exchanges, fewer battles over semantics. The Western Mountains first, then Quadril and its attached states, the Riverward, Bethem-and-Din, and the Eastern Seas.

Her hairpins scattered noisily across the slate. Strands of silver and dark brown sprung free, tickling Ania's face. The braid's rough tail swept the floor. She threw it back over her shoulder like a promise.

Her books would *not* be taken.

The Pressmen's minions would have to go through Ania first. Like her mentor before her. At least, Ania suspected that was what had happened.

Several years ago, at the start of each semester, books from other libraries had begun arriving, secreted at the bottoms of bags that otherwise contained the usual—students' clothing freshly mended, a date cake for a professor, various bolts of cloth and metals useful for paying the term ahead. Each time, the Master Archivist would pack her knapsack. "Another university is closing. We'll try to save their volumes."

In her absences, Ania covered Master Vos's classes.

More often than not, the older woman would return empty-handed. "Nothing left."

"I should have seen this coming," Ania muttered to the books. She'd been too busy trying to do her job, and Master Vos's too.

Decoys were what she'd bring to the meeting. Master Vos would be proud. Just enough books to sate the Pressmen—Ania hoped—while she preserved the library's treasures.

The early meeting, where Dean Andol would hand over the university's books, loomed like the sunrise. Ania tried to sort volumes into piles even faster. Dictionaries, diaries, catalogs, concordances, essays, letters, stories. Every volume precious enough to the past that someone had toiled over each page's words, whether hand-inked or typeset, the stitching, the binding.

Touching a book, for Ania, was like touching a person's fingertips across the years. She could feel a pulse, a passion for the knowledge the book contained.

Even the decoys.

She brushed the worn cover of one decoy volume—the fishing text. For each lost book, a connection silenced. Her fingers twitched before she pulled her hand back to her collarbone. Felt her own heart beating beneath the sweat-damp cloth.

No. Hesitation stole time better spent elsewhere.

In the predawn dark, Ania bent low beside the latest stack of books she'd decided to save. She tried to lift the stack, but it was too heavy. Instead, she braced her hands against the lowest volume, a thick work on the history of ink, and pushed the entire batch before her like a Far Reaches tugboat might push a mail scow. Slowly, she inched toward the wall that housed the library's distinctive clock. The clock's moon-shaped disc filled the main hall with its glow, the numbers etched shadow in its face and across the floor. The even *tick-tick-tick* and hourly chimes had been a constant friend to Ania since before the Master Archivist disappeared for the last time.

WAH-CHOO—Ania sneezed loudly. The sound rippled among the stacks.

Her foot slipped on one of the Pressmen's flyers: *Knowledge Unity: An Education for All—meeting at seven* A.M. She'd let them flutter to the floor. She sneezed again. Her long braid swung down and clung to the sweat on her face. Everything itched from the dust of books long unread, thousands of them, still in the stacks. Her decoy books might protect those too, for a time, as well as those she was hiding away.

She worked faster.

When the clock struck six, Ania smelled morning—clean and bright—on the ocean breeze. She slid open a door beneath the clock, revealing its secret maintenance room.

Before she ducked inside, she pushed the "keep" pile of books over the threshold.

There hadn't been enough room behind the clockwork for books to begin with. Not until she'd moved the Master Archivist's cot out into the archives. Now there was barely room for Ania to stand unless she crawled beneath the clockwork. She was trying to save too many books.

"How am I going to get any of you to safety?" she whispered.

The clock ticked an opaque response.

How indeed. And where? For many of these books, the last university in the Far Reaches had been a final hope.

Ania took another deep breath: old paper, leather and cloth bindings. The sharp rush of ink tickled her nose.

Her throat tightened at the thought of no one teaching her favorite books again.

She glanced up at the clock. At the lettering, hand-painted by the Master Archivist's grandmother, with whom she'd shared her name: Sonoria. At the numbers, in gold serif, each bigger than her head. Her foot crunched another flyer that had slid in with the books.

Conquer the Losses of Time with Knowledge.

Ania almost laughed, then worried she wouldn't be able to stop. Instead, she rebraided her hair, smoothing the snarls and tucking the loose bits back in.

As dawn broke across the clock face set high in the wall of the tiny room, Ania repinned the long braid so that it circled her head like a loose, gray-stranded crown. The Master had once told her that her brown eyes and sturdy chin balanced the look. "You are quiet, certainly, but you are respectable, responsible. With a kind of hidden fierceness." Ania hoped that fierceness would help her.

Less than respectable was her professor's robe. Second-tier professor's cords were attached with sure stitches, but the cream panels were dusty from being pressed to the library floor for so long. Patched from long wear, too, but that was Ania's fault, not the library's. The garment would not merit respect from the Pressmen or the deans, though they barely noticed her unless they needed something.

Ania kept mostly to the library; she'd practically grown up in one, reading next to her professor father as he prepared his lectures. She knew what to do here, what to say, and when to be quiet. She was good with students. And she'd kept from making too many connections in the swirl of academia because the library always felt safer. Having to step into this new role made her teeth ache.

Perhaps she could make herself presentable before the morning meeting, which was . . . She glanced at the backlit clock, its dark arms splayed against the opaque glass, its gears visible on both sides. At the shadow cast on the wall behind. The meeting was now.

"Silverfish and hordes," she breathed. She wished the old Master hadn't disappeared. She wished she had more guidance, more time.

She imagined the comforting ticks in the Master Archivist's voice, lecturing her: *Cleanliness is more important than rank.*

Ania paused, then nodded at the clock. "Fine, then."

She pulled off her cloak and turned it inside out. The dark lining looked much like an unadorned graduate's wrap, but at least it appeared clean.

Ania locked the clockroom behind her and carried the decoy books to the cart. When she returned, she would teach the Master's first class of the day: Research and Discontinuity Between Texts. The school had vowed to stay open as long as there were students.

She hoped the students were safe, that the Pressmen at the university gates would relent. Or that the deans' ploy would work.

~

The Last Meeting, as the morning would later be called among scattered academics, was more of a melee. Book-laden carts rested outside Gladulous Hall. Ania left her own cart at the crowd's edge, noting that she'd brought the fewest, and the shabbiest, where others' carts nearly overflowed.

So many books. Her fingers twitched as she wove her way between the piles.

As she entered Gladulous Hall, the crowd drew close around her, all waiting to get through the doors. The event had drawn more than faculty. Curious students, strangers from town. Ania could see nothing but shoulders and backs. More late arrivals pressed behind her until she was trapped there. Deep within the hall, a shout reverberated.

The crowd swayed, revealing a sky-colored banner overhead. Blue and white once signified the Western Mountains. Then, as the Western Mountains' army spread beyond the mountains, along with their weapons and technology, the colors became more ubiquitous. Especially when the Pressmen began using the colors on information about their printing press, their rules, and their *Compendiums*. And began wearing blue. Ania ground her teeth.

The sight of white and blue never failed to make her more stubborn. Her grandparents and parents had been the same way.

The crowd shifted. Ania's stubbornness increased at a swish of white and blue along the corridors. Two Pressmen stripped the robe from an art professor's shoulders and let the garment fall to the ground.

Ania's hopes sank in her stomach, suddenly heavy and sour.

The Pressmen hadn't been held back. More colleagues, from university guards to Dean Andol, already wore blue and white cloaks, or shiny metal pins in the shape of a book split open, the pages left smooth and blank.

Some students also wore Pressmen pins on their robes. They led a chorus of jeers now, against the professors.

"Share what you know, university staff! Too long you've kept the best from us and scoffed!"

"Masters of what's right, what's poor! Soon you won't decide anymore!"

Ania's breath caught. Among those yelling, one of the Master Archivist's favorite students and several of her first-year students. Their faces transformed by fear into masks of anger. She struggled to understand.

They're just children.

"Your departments have resisted the call for books until now," Dean Andol said, blinking nervously. His voice shook. That alarmed Ania the most.

"But the school has capitulated. And you have stepped forth to add your contributions, students and teachers both. There will be peace between academia and the Pressmen, at least at Far Reaches."

Curious students, still undecided, turned their heads to see how the faculty reacted.

How would children do otherwise? They'd been taught to follow others' examples here.

The speed with which professors threw in with the Pressmen worsened the sour taste in Ania's mouth.

"We should have done this earlier," said the head of

shipping and trade law. His voice was rough, but he pulled more books from his satchel, as if he'd known what was coming. Ania had often looked things up for him in the library. He'd always been polite.

Now he passed one of the books he'd borrowed from her to a Pressman in exchange for a book-shaped loyalty pin.

With speedy nods, several metals professors also took pins, former students too. Others who protested, even by shaking their heads, were pushed into a corner and held there by Pressmen. Their academic robes were thrown to the crowd, some of whom spit on the cloth.

Ania clutched her own satchel to her side. But no one demanded anything of her, except an occasional "move!"

In confusion, she looked down at her robes and remembered what she'd done.

Her professorial regalia hidden, her face still scuffed with dust, she was being treated like a student. She opened her mouth to protest, then shut it. Tugged on a sleeve to rumple her dark robes further.

Ania hated herself a little for that. If she'd been loyal to her persecuted colleagues, if she was any better than the metals professors, she should have reversed her robes. Pulled the twice-corded sleeves out and waved them in the faces of the tall, glass-faced guards.

But she didn't.

Ania, too, was reduced by the reality of the Pressmen's campaign. Her heart beat irregularly and too fast, itself trying to survive.

To survive, to keep going, to remember—she tried to quiet her fears. But a chill passed through her. Would there be a record of what happened here if the Pressmen controlled all the books? Would it really mean peace?

Ania's heart pounded faster. She would continue to try to keep some books out of the Pressmen's hands, to smuggle at least some far from the archipelago. A small revenge. Something her grandparents, and their parents, who'd fled Quadril and the Jeweled Valley long ago, would have appreciated.

Trapped within the press of student bodies, Ania started to panic. She needed to move quickly, before the Pressmen found her trove and destroyed it too.

Finally, a Pressman leader, wearing the color blue that Ania knew once heralded the Western Mountains' army, addressed the students. "You can join up with us, try for jobs in Quadril, or help distribute *Universal Compendiums* here. Either way, you'll soon be freed of the need for this place, peace or no. Soon enough, you'll have Knowledge wherever you go. Nothing will be out of reach for anyone." The speaker waved a hand. The students were dismissed.

They shifted uneasily and began to move to the door.

"Universities kept knowledge from those who couldn't afford it," a young man said behind Ania. "It hasn't been fair."

Head bowed, Ania began to move out of the hall with the crowd.

"We know there are professors still hiding more books." Dean Andol's voice carried over the students' whispers. "Find them, bring them here. If you do, you'll be cared for until you find work. We'll feed you, house you if you need it. Or we'll trade for your fare home. Exams are hereby canceled."

Ania didn't dare turn around as the students applauded. So Dean Andol had done more than agree to turn over the books. He'd capitulated the university.

The dean hadn't spotted her yet. Or, probably more likely, he'd never really seen her when they spoke. But she cheered with the rest of the students, a sour sound buoyed by fear. She was a student now, for all that this meant. A student of falsehood and lies, of survival and mean bargains.

Xachar Oubliant, one of Ania's first-year students, also didn't recognize her in the crowd. Turning her robes around had saved her. Meantime, Ania remembered Xachar. He'd borrowed several engineering books early in the semester and hadn't returned them yet. Now he'd pinned the badge of Pressman's senior helper to his robes.

He strained at the handles of an overflowing book cart, working to be the first to pull it forward to the part of the square where large crates waited.

Ania looked away fast, her heart pounding in her ears.

She kept walking. She moved forward in the crush of robes, her eyes on her shoes, on her fellow escapees' shoes. Brown leather, embroidered cloth, patched canvas. Her eyes blurred the seams with tears that didn't fall.

"Where are the rest of your books!" The shouts began. "No more hoarding knowledge!"

An engineering professor on his knees in the corner opened his mouth when he saw Ania. He'd greeted her often as they passed on the square with a cheerful "Librarian!" The engineer had always taken good care of the books he borrowed.

Would he betray her now? The professor clamped his lips shut. More loyal to her than she to him.

Ania took one step and then the next. An even pace, like a clock's tick.

Betrayal and lies.

The deans' lies. Her own betrayals.

Guilt bore Ania out of that hall and into the sunlight.

A few of the Master Archivist's first-year students sat on the library steps, the same place where they'd often waited for their lessons on ancient records and continuity problems. Now they looked like baby birds, gray and cowlicked in the morning light, peering from side to side, trying to figure out what was happening. Unwilling to leave, but unwilling to brave Gladulous Hall.

If Ania were to go to them, to take them into the library, the Pressmen might think her a professor. They might capture her then, and the books she'd saved. But already the Pressmen were fanning out over the campus square, rifling through the carts, grabbing professors and students alike who did not wear their pins, commandeering assistants. She had to help these students escape.

As Ania moved across the square with a student's measured pace, she glanced behind her. Two Pressmen pulled three professors to stools in the center of the square, before the crates. The professors looked outraged. The engineering professor seemed to be arguing. The Pressmen blew handfuls of dust in their faces.

Ania kept moving away from them, toward the library. *Forward. Keep going.*

But she couldn't help it. She looked back. The three professors slumped on their stools, faces pale, their eyes blank.

Forward, she commanded her feet. Only forward.

Up ahead, the students waited. If she turned away, they would be easily taken and given the same tasks as Xachar Oubliant.

Ania chose once more. She stepped quickly across the

remains of the square, parting the Pressmen and students in her way.

She opened the library's small door, which was not her usual way. Ania, like Master Vos before her, been known for swinging the big archive doors wide, an invitation.

Her students rose and reached for their knapsacks, wanting to ask questions. She stilled them with a finger to her lips.

"Librarian, stop!" The distant shout broke the morning. Dean Andol.

Ania kept moving. "Forward," she said to the door, the air, the library.

"Librarians who talk to empty shelves rather than listening to their colleagues will be left to their fate," Dean Andol shouted.

Ania pressed ahead. She did talk to the library. She listened too.

She heard the sound of running feet behind her.

Listening wasn't the same as obeying. Refusing to follow wasn't the same as being abandoned.

Ania waved the last student through the shadow of the library's archways instead. She shut and bolted the small door with a loud bang that echoed through the stacks.

No Pressmen would find her trove of books or conscript these students.

"Come down below." She beckoned her class. They

looked at her, surprised and hesitant—they'd never been in the library's basement. "It's safer."

She took a deep breath. Would they listen to her? "You must go home. Tell people what you saw here, but very carefully. You must not become part of this. You must remember."

When she'd begun traveling to rescue books, the Master Archivist had stored food in the basement and in the clockroom. Ania shared out some of the remaining biscuits and dried fruit with her students.

"I'll show you out the back way," she whispered. "Then run as far as you can. Don't stop to get your things from your rooms. Go home, hide your robes. Go."

The five students listened wide-eyed; they could sense that she'd told them a truth.

"Will you take some of these?" Ania held up a book, feeling guilty. These books might not make it, but then again, they might. Ania couldn't run them to safety on her own. But her students could.

When four students nodded, she tucked a book in each of their bags. Perhaps one or two books would survive.

Until there was nowhere left to hide the books that the Pressmen hadn't already found.

"If you're discovered, you may be able to trade the book for your freedom," she said. That eased her heart—she was giving them a way out of being caught, becoming Pressmen.

When the last student's shadow disappeared into the steam tunnels, Ania locked that passage too. The remaining books were too many and too heavy to carry.

She would stay. She would defend the library, at least until the students were well away from the Far Reaches.

She would become the decoy.

2

Jorit

Jorit Lee knew a dozen things. She knew when to get out and when to stay put. She knew six ways to pick a lock. And four ways to conceal her identity.

A lot of thieves knew these things.

The cart she rode in creaked and groaned loudly in the dawn quiet as they moved over the archipelago's last bridge. She shifted, trying to spare her bones the jostle. The Pressmen had sailed to the Far Reaches from the Eastern Seas, while Jorit took the more bruising path.

"Metalsmith, eh?" the cart driver said.

Jorit shrugged. She'd hung a jeweler's loupe around her neck. She fiddled with it as the cart driver attempted conversation. It belonged to her grandfather, long ago.

Thieves knew a lot of things, but expertise—finesse—that was more important than knowing, most times. And Jorit's expertise was being inconsequential.

She and her brother Marton had followed the Pressmen's path across the Six Kingdoms once their studies abruptly ended. *Safer to be in the Pressmen's wake than between them and what they wanted*, Marton had reasoned more than once.

They'd found ways to make a small profit here and there. They'd changed their clothes, their looks, their methods, and they'd only rarely been caught. The thief's mark carved on her hand in Quadril had begun to fade to a pale scar.

As the kingdoms unified, Jorit knew it was vitally important to fade, to fit in. Once everyone knew what set an individual apart, the more they seemed to desire its elimination.

Jorit ruffled her fingers through her close-cropped, shoe-blacked hair. She missed the fingerless gloves she'd had in Quadril, but they'd worn through. With few ways to hide the mark, and none to clear her name, she was a thief on the run, and would always be so. Her scalp itched from the dye job, but with it and a change of clothes, she'd been able to pass herself off as a local student. At least from a distance, in the shadows. If she kept her hands tucked in her sleeves.

Quadril and then the Eastern Shores had changed how they traveled: Marton not at all, and Jorit in faster, more desperate ways. She was running out of kingdoms, and without Marton, she had no plan. Instead, she had a singular need to keep moving, and a sense that it was safer to do so alone. And if Jorit couldn't get back what she'd lost, she knew she'd settle for safety.

"They may not have use for you for long at the university," the cart man said. His horse snorted steam into the sea-salted air. "Seeing as everyone will be able to learn anything they want from one book soon. No more students. No more teachers."

Jorit bit her tongue. She'd heard this argument before. When the Pressmen came, this philosophy always came with them. More and more, people welcomed it.

Marton had always been the one to try to explain the difference between being told a thing was true and experiencing the truth of it firsthand. And at first, he'd been all for the Pressmen's goals. *Access to books and information should be easier than it is in the Six Kingdoms,* he'd said while they studied late at night. *We shouldn't have to fight so hard to learn.* She'd asked him then, *But do people value it more when they have to fight for it?* Jorit could hear their younger voices bantering in her memory. She shook her head to clear it.

She'd stick with the safer way from now on. She raised her voice so the cart man could hear her over the sound of its wheels. "I expect so."

The cart creaked to a stop before the university gates. A group of Pressmen approached, asking the driver about the contents of his cart. *Did he have any books?* They offered a very pretty sum.

The driver shook his head, then turned to point to Jorit. But she was already gone.

~

Jorit watched the Pressmen set off the last of the strange charges they'd brought.

As the buildings of the Far Reaches' only remaining university began to collapse under their own weight and sink into their foundations, Jorit made mental lists of things she could recover and sell from the structures still standing.

In the arts building, all she'd found were metal bindings, palette knives. A few notebooks. Everything else had been picked over already.

The good jewelry was long gone. And everyone in the Far Reaches suddenly seemed to have plenty of knives.

She'd waited far too long. She hadn't waited long enough.

But the library still stood. And it might still have books, if the doors had remained locked for days, as everyone was saying. Last night, she'd heard Pressmen returning to their barracks—former dormitories—muttering about going inside. Wondering at missing colleagues who'd tried to enter and not returned. This morning, she heard more returning in a group: a flock of young assistants, led by a guide.

"Historically, universities never even enriched the towns they occupied. They kept all their best knowledge locked inside their walls. The Pressmen have always fought to share that knowledge equally," the guide was saying. "Now that we have the technology, we're able to do that far faster. What was once a small protest against academic fortresses? Is now changing the Six Kingdoms for the better."

The new assistants nodded in the dawn.

"So go out today and find as many hidden books as possible. Buy what you can to keep people happy. Take the rest. If you find a professor, call for help. We'll free these words from what binds them. We'll share everything. And then we'll level the rest."

With excited shouts, the assistants scattered across the square. Jorit's eyes followed the guide to where he took up a seat next to the crates. She heard his purse jingle, filled with money.

Even pieces of books could attract a buyer. Blank books brought less, but still paid. Jorit had sold some sketchbooks from the arts building already. *Sell a few books from the library,* she thought in the dark shadow of the university's wall, *and escape the Far Reaches for good.*

And go where?

Some of the outer islands beyond the Far Reaches. The ones without any universities. Jorit knew they were too small for the Pressmen, for now. But passage was expensive. Giving up was more affordable.

Over the wall, a sooner bird spit a warning: *Te-la! Te-LA!*

Jorit jumped. *Stop thinking like that.*

But she knew the pattern by now. Scholars dedicated to maintaining individual universities felt strong before the Pressmen arrived. They took in fleeing students. Shepherded more books inside their walls. Idealists held on until the Last Meeting. A few hard-core academics in each kingdom stayed through the inevitable Declaration Against Information Hoarding to make sure their students got home all right. A few more would flee. Some might be trapped, eventually, among the leveled buildings. She didn't like to think of that.

Jorit had learned the pattern at other universities the Pressmen visited. Once they began weakening buildings and setting charges, Jorit readied her bags. First the administration and lecture halls. The arts building. The library.

Jorit touched a finger to the Pressmen pin she'd stolen. She'd abandoned her pretense that she was a researcher, a metalsmith, a student, a refugee from another university.

These identities were no longer necessary. They were dangerous.

It had been true, once. Metalsmith first class with a focus on gems, until the Pressmen demanded her research, especially on the mythical Jeweled Valley. Accused her and Marton, both, of stealing jewelers' tailings when they refused to comply. Marked them as thieves.

So marked, they'd become just that.

Now Jorit was determined to escape. She knew the cost of staying too long, far too well. She knew the price of a ship's berth. Or had known it yesterday. It had probably doubled now.

A week ago, the territories firmly under the Pressmen's control seemed a lot safer than the places they were still trying to take over. But now, for the first time in Jorit's life without Marton, the Pressmen held every kingdom. She could no longer stay one step ahead of them, or follow behind them either. They were no longer on the move. They just were.

But the ocean was still free. Jorit sniffed at the sea air hungrily. Maybe she'd stay out there for good this time. No one to mind her out there.

And no one to mind, either. She ground her teeth. *Mustn't think about that.*

Her stomach ached as she shouldered her nearly empty canvas knapsack, the metal buckles on the straps clinking gently together. Her feet crunched on the seashell-flecked paving stones.

Jorit moved from the shadows into the dusty dawn light. She hadn't eaten in a while, but she had gotten used to an empty belly.

A person could get used to almost anything in order to survive.

Her soft leather boots crunched on the gravel from one of a dozen sunken buildings as she sped toward the library, taking the shortest way possible. Aside from the assistants, few people were out this early. Far Reaches hadn't been a big university to begin with. It had merely been the *last* university.

The archipelago had been cut off from much of the Six Kingdoms for a year once the Pressmen had joined with the forces from the Western Mountains and consolidated power along the border of Quadril. Thus strengthened, the movement focused its sights on the islands.

Despite the blockade, many resources from other universities in the Six Kingdoms had made their way to free shores. So Jorit had done the same. She'd been safe for a while. Then, days ago, she'd watched Far Reaches professors and students concede their books to the Pressmen.

The guards had taken piles of books and papers from every division. What came next, she didn't want to be here to see.

But Jorit moved too slowly.

As she headed for the library, the first charges boomed, and the building slumped, then settled lower.

She covered her eyes and nose. Waited for the cloud of dust to clear. Some of the building still stood. A charge must not have detonated.

Jorit inched closer to the foundation. Saw several blue-clad Pressmen staring at a wall. She slipped back around the other way, toward the collapsed side. Best to stay back.

"Metalsmith?" A whisper came from a half-buried window by her feet.

Jorit jumped and then peered warily into the darkness. "Who is there?" She wasn't a metalsmith anymore, but she still wore the colors. Fine. She'd be safer if someone remembered her clothes, which she could replace, rather than something she couldn't: her hands.

It wasn't safe to be memorable now. She reached for one of her knives. A sharp one.

"Name's Xachar. I'm stuck."

Xachar—the name wasn't that of a Far Reaches native. The voice was a young man's. He'd recognized her cloak as being that of a metalsmith, so he might have been a student once. But on his one visible sleeve, he wore a Pressmen's patch. Not a pin, a real patch. Roughly sewn, so newly vowed.

Was he one of the Pressmen that had supposedly gone missing? Would his rescue give Jorit a reward? Or would it get her caught? "Why are you here, Pressman?"

She'd learn as much as she could. But then, maybe, the knife.

She was pretty sure she could use it. She'd come close.

"I was getting a few things to help my brother buy passage. Faked loyalty to the Pressmen to do it." He looked at his patch, then back to Jorit. "I was in the stacks, and I got stuck. When the doors were locked from the other side. I don't like tight spaces. And then they set the charges."

So Xachar had had the same idea as Jorit, but worse luck. His reasons, though. He reminded her of her own brother, a little. *Marton.* Her heart still ached.

"I'll help you," she said. She looked for a way inside.

"I can see a light," Xachar said, struggling. "It's flickering, like there's fire deep in the stacks. Other Pressmen have disappeared in here already. I don't want to be among them. Please hurry."

Pressmen disappearing in the library. So it was true. Must be why they hadn't sacked the stacks yet, just leveled it.

Jorit sped up her search for an entrance, finally slipping under a door to one of the building's former steam tunnels, hidden beneath a pile of broken masonry. The

Pressmen hadn't found this yet. But Jorit and Marton had been the Quadril mining school's neediest students. They hadn't always had the money to pay for classes, or books. So they'd learned the value of a good steam tunnel years ago for getting into libraries after hours.

She laughed bitterly. *Now everyone would have the same information, about everything. And soon I might be the only person left who doesn't much want that anymore.*

But that was how she liked it now. Alone, you didn't stand to lose as much.

Hurry. Her knees and palms ground against the broken masonry. The dust from the other buildings' falls had settled on everything. The building smelled like chalk and dirt. Her teeth felt gritty, and she kept sneezing.

She tied a sturdy rope—her latest good find—to the nearest pole. Double hitched it. Then kept moving.

Always keep moving. That's the only safe way. Her brother's advice, and she'd listened, every time but once. *Don't risk yourself for others.* She knew that one too.

When she came through the rakish angles created by the stacks' fall, she toggled her lantern's switch. A small cloud of acrid carbide slowly faded into a glow. She saw holes in walls where doorways had split and shelving had toppled.

The lantern swung a wild arc of light against the walls. Jorit was a spider. A thief. A monster.

She swallowed hard. Whatever it took to survive.

"Xachar?" she called softly. "I'm coming around to you. Make some noise so I know which way." She could get him out before the Pressmen caught them. She knew it.

Not like Marton. She hadn't been able to do that.

She thought could hear the boy whimpering somewhere very nearby.

"Almost to you," she said. But she thought, *As fast as I can, before we're both caught.*

She'd be caught as a thief. Made an example of, like the professors. Go missing. Like her brother.

Jorit climbed over the thin bones of one of the library's metal shelves, its contents tumbled beneath it. A wooden container slid from a corner as her feet made the shelves sway again, and dust rose.

She held her breath, trying not to sneeze.

Xachar crouched halfway out and halfway in the building a few stacks away. His long black hair spilled down his back, loosened from the clip he'd used to pin it; his student's tunic was torn, the skin beneath scratched with angry red welts.

When Jorit moved the shelving that had pinned him, he groaned in relief.

"You all right?" she asked. In the lantern's light, it was hard to distinguish the younger man's expression:

Stunned? Confused? He almost looked pleased to see her. It was hard to tell. Could be in shock, Jorit decided.

Xachar looked behind him and down, so she couldn't see his expression. "I cut my arm." He held up his left forearm. Bandaged with a torn strip of Xachar's robe, the wound was slowly blooming red through the off-white piece of cloth, staining the Pressmen's badge.

"I found an easier way out, if you think you can make it." She held up the rope end. "You just need to follow this line."

He was so young. But serious. Like Marton had been, back in Eastern Shores. And hurt.

Jorit waited as Xachar considered the rope. "I can manage. It's just a scratch. Being trapped was harder."

The boy slid unsteadily to the library floor. He followed Jorit through the twists and turns, out of the tight space.

Jorit didn't see any fire as they walked. The boy must have been seeing things in his panic.

"You'll be all right." Jorit put her hand on Xachar's uninjured arm. "Get going. Before it's too late."

Xachar's already large brown eyes widened considerably. "You're staying? But . . . if you're caught . . ." He was staring at her hand.

Jorit blinked. Had the boy seen the thief's mark? She hadn't been careful enough.

"I cut myself once, but . . ." She began to try to explain away the mark, to claim it wasn't the archaic symbol but something else, but realized he was staring at her books. "But nothing. Here. Take these." She gave Xachar the last three sketchbooks she'd found in the arts building. "Get your brother and go."

"What about you?" the boy said, his voice less afraid, more distant. Probably thinking of his own brother, Jorit decided.

"I can get more books, and I won't get caught. I'll be at the docks soon enough." Marton had once said the same thing, and she'd believed him, right up until she'd seen the Pressmen carrying his limp form away. But today, she'd done a good thing. Helped someone else escape. Jorit breathed a little easier. That counted for something.

As Xachar's footsteps receded, she turned back to search the stacks. From the corner of her eye, near what was once the main hallway, she spotted a glimmer of light. Perhaps the young man had been right about a fire after all.

If it was fire, all remaining treasures here would be destroyed. Then it really would be too late for Jorit to get out. She'd given away part of her boat money. *Stupid.*

There was time, perhaps, to see how bad the fire was, and whether it was easily extinguished. *Let there be valu-*

able books left, Jorit thought. *Please let them be enough for passage.*

As she drew closer, dust curled up from the floor. She quickly covered her nose and mouth. She'd seen what the Pressmen's dust could do, out in the square, and in many university squares before that.

But she smelled no fire yet, heard no roaring crackle, sensed no great heat. And they still grumbled above over the charges. She had time.

Water dripped from a cracked pipe to her left, softly repetitive splashing sounds on the strewn floor.

Water. Bad for books and artifacts. Good for putting out fires.

The dust-saturated air thickened as Jorit walked. Light flickered in the hallway, wavering on the ceiling. At first she thought it was fire too.

The clock, cracked and its numbers nearly gone, reflected wavering sunlight onto the library's slate floor across its broken face. Jorit relaxed. The boy had been wrong.

"You said it was safe here."

Jorit jumped as a muffled voice broke the silence. Not Xachar's voice.

She moved toward the light, balancing silently on the balls of her feet.

Used to be, a person walked like that so as not to scare

the mice in the halls after dark. Not to get caught reading in locked libraries.

Now she was still trying to not get caught.

Jorit touched her fingers to the haft of her own blade. It wasn't much. But it was hers.

The soles of her shoes whispered against the dust and torn paper on the floor. *Ledge,* said one shred. *Know,* said another.

Behind the clock's face, light flickered. Not sunlight. Reflected shadows licked at a corner from outside. Now she smelled flint. She heard a triumphant yell.

They'd finally fixed the errant charge. It was too late.

She'd known better. She ducked into a small room beneath the clock as more charges went off. The rest of the library shook and fell deeper into its foundations.

3.

Ania

The day after she'd locked the library, the floor rattled beneath Ania's feet. Doors banged against their frames, and the windows clattered. Then the ground under the library shook, and heavy shelves toppled over in the stacks. The last of Ania's hairpins chimed against the floor, her braid once again undone and swinging free.

Her "to-save" books rustled and slid, a few tumbling open on the clockwork room floor. She hustled to restack them, to preserve their spines, their bindings.

The clock kept a steady beat, smoothing her calm, even as more blue and white uniforms moved back and forth near the windows, more Pressmen set up camp in the university square. They served the remaining students meals, gave speeches about Knowledge. Occasionally a Pressman would lift a piece of greenish glass out of a bag and set it on the ground. When they picked it up again later, the sunlight would strike it, but the glass wouldn't reflect the light. It had turned dark as ink.

The students, too, had changed. They'd become willing assistants, taking in the Pressmen's philosophy. Ania couldn't judge them for that. In return for food, they'd packed books in crates without complaint. They hadn't looked at the fallen buildings, only at the Pressmen who set the charges, who carried the crates away.

Ania, peeking out through the library windows, watched for more professors, but didn't see any.

With Pressmen everywhere, she sequestered herself once again in the clockroom. The clock's beat surrounded her, comforted her. As the buildings disappeared one by one, she passed more time there each day, trying to memorize books, to bear their words away in her head if she had to.

"The valley gems numbered eighty-five at their peak, including the Immaculate Stone, the Steadfast Diamond, the Star Cabochon . . . ," she whispered. She traced the drawings of each gem's setting with her fingers. "No unset gem should be trusted," she read. "No setting should be soldered without careful thought to pressure and use."

The clock sometimes stuttered like a laugh, and she'd oil the workings. Ania laughed with the clock. She been going a little crazy, memorizing. But she felt safe here.

She was fairly sure Pressmen had come into the clockroom once already, and even more sure that the clockroom had kept her safe.

Truth was, Ania was still trying to get her head around what had happened. She'd heard footsteps. Shouts. Someone had tried to break into the clockroom, and then—

No. She couldn't—she hadn't been hurt, but she still couldn't—it was as if a fog had passed over her memories.

Think, Ania. If she was going mad, she needed to know. Being trapped in the library for even a few days without all her faculties was dangerous. *Think. What do you remember?*

Pressmen had entered the library. She'd hidden in the clockroom, shored up the door with a barricade of books, then climbed into the gears, up a small spiral staircase made of brass, and perched there, waiting.

She wished she'd thought to get a weapon. She'd sworn to protect the books. But she was a teacher, not a fighter. She'd sparred a little in primary school, but that was it. All she had now were hairpins.

And the Pressmen saw the barricade's edge beyond the broken door— A pile of books! Treasure! She'd been so stupid. They decided to investigate. When they pushed through the door, the helmeted fighters didn't spot Ania, kneeling high in the clockwork. Not at first.

Ania's muscles tensed with the strain of keeping still,

of not crying out in anger as a Pressman pocketed one book, then another.

She must have made some sound, because the Pressman turned toward where she cowered. Their gloved hand rested for a moment on the clockwork as they bent close, peering up.

That was where things got strange. She found it hard to remember what happened next.

Ania's heart pounded loud, or the clock did. The small, dark room drew close around her and then everything went black. She dreamed of strange places with terrible drums beating.

When she came to, clutching the railing of the spiral stair and cursing her own fear and weakness, the Pressmen were gone, but many of her books remained.

There was a small bit of blood on the floor beside the clockwork. But no body. Had she done something?

Ania couldn't remember. "I should get out," she whispered. No one answered. The clock ticked steadily.

But she hesitated, thinking of the damp walls along the steam tunnels, the prospect of emptiness, or Pressmen, on the other side. *What if everyone has already given up?*

Her colleague's face as he knelt on the floor of Gladulous Hall. She couldn't turn away from her memory of that.

When the floor rattled again, another loud boom followed. This one much closer. The sound drove air hard against the library's windows, against Ania's ears. The air pushed grit and dust through the clockwork, under the door, everywhere. It knocked Ania to the ground. Her teeth rang from the impact. She heard shelves begin to fall in the stacks.

She righted herself, slowly, for her vision swam. Her carefully stacked, hidden books had toppled. She reached for the nearest book, her ears still clanging. The cover torn, the title—a catalog of propriety from the Western Mountains—half missing. She held a sleeve over her mouth against the dust as she carefully smoothed the pages with her free hand, then placed the book back on the pile.

Another cloud of dust puffed between the clock's seals.

Light tilted and shone through the clock wall at a slightly different angle. Ania coughed at the dust and went out to investigate.

"Time preserve us," she whispered as she looked through the library's shuttered windows. Where Gladulous Hall had been, beyond the Pressmen's feast, only a roof showed above the ground.

"You no longer need these buildings," a Pressman shouted on the square.

A few students—former students now—and all the Pressmen cheered.

When Ania rested her head against the clockwork's metal gears, she could hear noise in the steam tunnels, rustling outside. She pressed her ear close.

"There are still books inside the library, and at least one thief!" a familiar voice said. Xachar. Her first-year student.

Mutters of disgust echoed through the metal. "We should make them carry the books out," someone said. "Whoever's still inside. That's safer than losing more of our people."

"Nah. The gems will do the work now," another voice near the door replied. "Once the words are gone, and their buildings are collapsed, the academics will give up and come stand with the rest of us."

Ania pressed her face against the clock glass, looking out between the letters *O* and *N* of *Sonoria Vos*. Gems? The word tickled her memory. A spark glowed across the square in the dim evening light. Moments later, another boom. A wall of dust went up around the arts building, and the ground rippled again. *No.*

When the air cleared, that building, too, was nearly gone—only its roof showed beside the smooth expanse of the square.

The Pressmen were using charges to sink the university into the ground, one building at a time, and gems to destroy the books somehow. Erasing the school and its books. *Including the library.*

Perhaps the clockroom would be buried deep within the earth. And—unless the ocean came for it—someday discovered again. A trove of books saved by time. Her bones left to guard it.

She didn't want to die here. She began to pack her satchel to head for the steam tunnels. But too late, more rustling. Shadows moved across the shuttered windows beyond the cracked clock face. The Pressmen's assistants called to one another as they set charges. Student cloaks flickered past among the blue and white.

She was trapped.

With the books, then. How fitting.

Ania hunkered down in the clockroom.

"We'll be all right. We will," she whispered.

She paused again. Listened.

The clock ticked irregularly. *Unless that's my heart?*

Whatever it was, the sound was reassuring.

"I believe you," she whispered.

She ducked farther into the clockwork, bending low, then climbed into the safety of the clockwork's winding staircase and covered her head with her arms.

As if they were amplified by the clock's curved glass, she could hear sounds from outside. Flint clicked. Fuses hissed.

Her heart or the clock stuttered as more charges went off. Ania heard only muted blasts this time, as if the clockwork protected her. The library shook and dropped deeper into the sediment. The clockroom, with its thick metal gears and stays, swayed but somehow remained intact.

She'd been right.

Her ears popped when the building settled. Dark gray dust puffed under the door and settled across the tops of the piles. Ania held her breath. More gray dust climbed the clock face beyond the wall.

Ania knelt on the spiral stairs, aware of her heart pounding in her ears.

She was still alive. She felt her arms and legs in the darkness, and couldn't find any injuries. She blinked, she felt no less aware than she had before. She started to congratulate herself on her luck, on the wisdom of the clockroom's builder.

But the library teetered, settling in its foundation. Before Ania could react, the clock's glass face cracked and the lower half crashed to the floor. The staircase groaned and began to twist. She jumped free. Landed hard on the floor, where a cold, sea-salted breeze kicked up dust.

The clockroom door didn't shut properly against the outside any longer. The enormous clock's gears bent when the staircase to access them finally fell.

She wept at that loss, above everything.

Worse, out the door, she could see the fallen half of the clock's face blocking the steam tunnels. Ania was truly trapped.

"You couldn't just leave, could you." Ania looked at the library where she'd spent her entire career, at the clock and books she loved. She leaned back against a wall, crooked now, and stared. Was everything lost?

The books she'd kept safe from the Pressmen. Were they still all right? *Check, Ania, before giving up entirely.*

The torn title page of the first book on the spilled pile was blank. So too the second book she lifted. Each book she picked up that had been touched by the dust was missing letters and words. Pools of ink ran from the piles down to the floor, leaving folios of blank paper.

As she watched, the pool of ink began to snake up the wall and out a crack in the nearest sunken window. In the distance far above, she could see a Pressman holding up a green stone that slowly turned black.

The clock's base, which had fallen in the blast, suffered in its new place on the floor. The seven and eight on its face had begun running down the clock face; the six was already gone. The name of its designer, which had formed a sweeping curve below the six? Gone too.

And with it, the Master Archivist's name. Gone.

"Sonoria," Ania whispered, as if finally saying good-bye. "Sonoria Vos." Her voice cracked on the last syllable. She held her fingers up to the blank glass where Sonoria's ancestor had once signed her name as the clock's designer.

And now both were lost.

When she drew her fingers back, she held her breath and carefully wiped the vestiges of dust—gritty stuff, like ground stones—from her skin.

With a groan, Ania dug deep into the stacks of books she'd salvaged, carefully moving those still legible out of reach of the dust on the ground. Only those volumes at the pile's center survived, and then only in the clockroom. If she ventured out into the library's wreckage, in search of her food cache or water from a leaking pipe, and got the least amount of dust on her hands or clothes, touching one of these had the same consequences.

The words ran from the page beneath her fingers, onto the floor, and away.

"No. No, this is not safe. You said it would be safe here." Ania jumped at the sound, then realized it was her own voice. Her own panic. Echoing through the small room, bouncing off the broken gears.

Nothing responded to her, not even the clock. She bit her lip to keep from saying more.

If anyone had been watching, they'd have seen Ania

seeming to fold up into herself, drawing in the quiet, taking shallow, tearing breaths, as she began to set her own words aside.

It would be so easy to give up. To climb from the library and let the Pressmen outside take the remaining books away. Take her away, too.

From the now-quieter library.

But something inside the clock—a beautiful marbled thing wound with gold wire that gleamed now in the shadows—kept ticking softly. She knelt closer to the clockwork, the sound comforting her until she calmed and started to think logically. She had water from the cistern. A cache of food still remaining from what she'd laid in when the trouble started.

The clock might be broken, but the fact that a part of it was still ticking made Ania feel better.

Then, a groan came, near the broken glass by a half-buried window. Far from where Ania stood.

Someone else was in the clockroom.

A shadow played against the wall.

"Who's here?" Ania called. *Another Pressman?*

"I got caught here," a woman's voice answered. A foot stepped on broken glass.

"Stay back," Ania cried. She reached for a shard of the clock's arm. Wondered whether this intruder would disappear like the others, if they got too close.

"*Necessity,*" she whispered. "Get away from me. From my books."

The figure who rose from the shadows was smaller than Ania. Younger. Her skin gleamed with dust and sweat. She sheathed her knife with a dramatic gesture. "I'm a student here. Trapped like you. I won't harm you."

Ania blinked. No one was a student here any longer. Or everyone was. She squinted at the woman. "I don't recognize you." Her jaw tightened. Had she seen the young woman at the meeting? Was she with the Pressmen now? "What's your name?"

"Jorit Lee. Came to the mining department after discovering that all the gems I'd studied were lost or broken, like the old gems. Not one real valley gem to be found any longer." Jorit rambled, her hands stuck in her pockets—perhaps out of shock at finding someone else here, or because she'd hit her head during the fall. Ania thought her smile was that of someone who'd seen their studies meet the real world and be crushed by it. Who had lost something. "Not that it matters."

Ania shook her head, confused. Would this person disappear too?

"How long have you been down here?" Jorit asked, moving closer.

Ania knew dust clotted her braid alarmingly. Her clothes smelled rank and smoky. Dirt lined the creases in her olive skin, and the loose librarian's robe, second tier, might have once been parchment toned but now was a mottled mushroom color, no matter whether she turned it inside out or not.

"A few days. Since the trouble started."

Jorit ran her fingers through her dark hair. Her hands came away smudged with black. "You came down here to guard the books." Surprise echoed into the stacks, a little louder than it should have been. On the back of one hand, Ania saw a pale scar. A thief's mark.

"I had to protect them, and the students," Ania said in a warning tone. She would continue to protect the books. She tried to look fierce. *There is absolutely nothing more to explain.*

She thought she saw a glimmer of understanding in the thief's eyes.

Jorit's fingers brushed a small, glittering leather-bound book beside her that rested on a stack of books. She didn't look at the broken, erased clock face at all.

"Leave that alone," Ania said.

To her surprise, Jorit lifted her hand from the book. Ania pulled it to her, carefully.

There was a long pause as the two sized each other up. "What are you doing here?" Ania finally asked again.

"Looking for anything I could sell to escape the Far Reaches," was Jorit's quick response. It was also an honest response, Ania felt. "If you've found anything good, we can try to get you out too, before the Pressmen come here again. Now that they know there are still books in here, they will."

"I'm not leaving," Ania said. She was sure of it now. The clockroom would protect her. "And I'm not a thief."

She gripped the book tighter in one hand, the piece of the clock's sweep hand in the other.

"We are all thieves now." The other woman—the thief—looked at her carefully. "Are you injured?"

"I'm not injured," Ania replied steadily. "And you're not stealing these. Any of them." She tightened her fingers around the sharp metal.

"Who's going to keep them? Where would you hide all these books?" Jorit scoffed, ignoring Ania's threat. "There's nowhere anymore. The Pressmen are glad to have them, more than anything. Supposedly their *Compendiums* require paper that's been used before, and ink too."

"No. I keep them safe. And they are not just paper and ink." Ania lifted Jorit's bag from her shoulder and looked inside. "Including these."

"No." Jorit reached for the bag. But loud footsteps clattered across the outer library hall. Both women fell silent and stared back where Jorit had come from.

"I'm telling you, thieves! Here, and worse. I can hear

them. They survived the collapse. Down there." A young man's voice.

The clockroom held its breath. "You led them here!" Ania finally whispered as the footsteps kept coming closer.

"I didn't—" Jorit groaned. She rubbed at the mark on her hand, her head turned. Listening.

Thieves and worse. "You recognize a voice?" Ania certainly recognized it.

This Jorit had succeeded where all the others had failed—luring her out, bringing danger with her. Ania knew that whatever it had done to the Pressmen, the clockroom couldn't protect her from a crowd.

A softer voice wound down the hall like fear. "The boy says we'll find the librarian down in here somewhere. And a thief with a book-filled knapsack."

"Xachar," Jorit groaned. "Why?"

Ania did the same. Though she'd been right about the voice, she couldn't get over her surprise. Her own student. Why indeed? "You didn't lead them here," she finally acknowledged. "But one of my former students, a Pressman now, has traded your kindness for a badge." She hissed.

"He's not a Pressman. He was trying to help his brother." Jorit sounded so sure.

"Xachar once told me he had no family to speak of.

That he was alone. That the university was all he had."
Ania saw Jorit's face fall.

The librarian made a fast decision and put the sweep hand down. She grabbed a few more books and put Jorit's stack back in her arms. If Jorit was in danger, perhaps she could be enticed to help hide books in exchange for a place to hide.

"Come on. Hurry. Be careful." Ania pointed deep into the clockwork as the guards shouted back and forth across the library's ruins. The thief looked at her, then down at her armful of books.

"Here's a food cache!" one guard shouted, much closer than Ania wanted.

"A cot. And a pile of books with print still on all the pages," another cried.

"Grab those."

"*No*," Ania whispered. "*Not more words lost.*" But she couldn't save them alone. She didn't want to count on this woman—a thief!—but she needed the help. "Please," she said.

"I'm with you." Jorit held the books in her arms tighter and followed Ania into the clockwork. "Where are we going?"

Ania smiled, grateful despite herself. Perhaps until the danger passed, it would be all right to let one person in.

"Somewhere safe." It was an uneasy truce. A thief and a librarian against the Pressmen. Would it be enough?

Against her better judgment, Ania pulled them both as close as possible to the clock's smaller case. The one that still ticked softly.

She remembered now.

They hid behind the small case, which she'd seen the Pressmen touch before everything went dark and a Pressman had disappeared.

~

Inside the clockwork, broken gears that had once ticked minutes, hours, and days stuck at odd angles.

Special bezels for lunar and solar calendars, and another for ancient harvest that meant nothing to the Far Reaches but must have once, were also still. From the back, these gears and bezels bore the handwritten notes of another watchman who had tended the clock: the previous Master Archivist.

But the clock was cracked. Once, Ania had held its broken sweep arm like a sword. She set her books down and eyed the broken casing. If she touched it, would she disappear too? Her hand wavered.

One tiny component continued to tick a familiar pattern inside the small room.

With the broken gears bent the way they were, Jorit stared at a brass casket deep enough in the workings that it was usually out of reach. The clock's heart glowed, exposed. Still ticking.

From the casket's back, connecting wheels had run to the larger clock, providing it with power.

Still glowing. Wrapped in a clockwork of its own.

"Is that a jewel?" When Jorit came too close, Ania moved to stand in front of it, still brandishing the sweep arm. "If this can help the two of us defend against the Pressmen"—Jorit pointed at the glow—"give it to me or grab it yourself!"

"I'll not give it to you. Jewelry? In a library? You're a thief, not a defender of words." Ania sounded surer than she felt. But she tried to block the brass casket anyway. She didn't want another person to disappear.

Her elbow jostled the casing. She didn't disappear.

Like the clockroom door, the casket swung open slightly at Ania's touch. While Jorit glanced between the clockwork and the barricade, Ania pulled the casket open to view the smaller clock—contained in a metal box the size of a large man's hand—hanging from a chain. A wheel connected at the back ran through the casket and into the clockwork.

This still turned.

Ania touched the worn metal case of the smaller timepiece, and the clock dropped out. Right into the thief's hands.

The librarian gasped and reached for the clock. Jorit gripped it tightly, and then they both held it, the metal momentarily slick against their fingers even as the movements beat regular in their grasps.

"You broke it!" Jorit worried.

"It was already broken," Ania replied. "The Master never told me what drove the clock, and I never thought to ask. I guess this is it."

The shouting grew louder as the soldiers finally entered the main hall and began pressing on the broken door. Ania heard a dog snuffling, then a whine.

"Here!" a guard shouted, her voice twisted by a Far Reaches lilt.

The guards peering around the door wore the same gear as the Pressmen Jorit had spotted outside. Helmets, blue and white uniforms. Batons drawn and hands laden with bags of dust.

"Come out!"

"Immediately!"

Jorit grasped Ania's hand as the Pressmen pushed against the door. Ania recoiled at first—the gall of this stranger, this thief—and then clutched Jorit's hand back. They were in this together, at least for now. The clock glowed brighter.

Jorit almost dropped the small clock as it became warm, but Ania steadied that too.

It isn't safe here, the clock seemed to tick.

In their fingers, the timepiece that had long driven the entire mechanism for the library's clockwork ticked quietly, a comforting few seconds. Those ticks spread out like ripples, each one taking longer. Sweeping up against the broken brass gears.

"It's not safe here," Ania said, echoing the clock.

The ticks from the timepiece drowned out Jorit's reply.

They became louder, a road of them, a trail down which her mind was drawn, a tunnel, an escape hatch.

"Are we dying?" Ania whispered. "Is my heart giving in? Am I—" Panic built, and the clock no longer calmed her.

Jorit's scarred hand held steady against hers and the clock's warming metal.

And the library—the library was dissolving into swirls of dust and shadow all around them. The broken brass door and the gears were the last to go.

Beyond where they stood, there was nothing. No guards, no passages of toppled books skewed through the stacks. Ania bit a scream between her teeth.

The dust thickened to a cloud that closed around everything, and the clock's ticking went on for what seemed like one long minute, then another, before the minutes seemed to pile upon one another and skip around.

First Jorit, then Ania tripped on uneven ground and landed in thick river mud.

Behind them, flames danced across the walls of a palace built in a very old style. There was a beat of drums unlike anything Jorit had ever heard.

"Where are we?" Jorit had time to gasp. An arrow flew past Ania's head.

4.

Xachar

When the two women in the library disappeared, Xachar Oubliant searched desperately through the bent gears, the tumbled shelves.

He'd promised his squad leader he'd find the last academics hiding in the university, as well as books. The senior Pressmen would tire of him if he wasn't useful, he knew. And Xachar wanted to be useful, to gain a better position, as he'd been promised.

But he'd failed at being a guide. His squad of students hadn't found as many professors as they'd been assigned. They hadn't found many books either, until the library. And none of his group had been willing to go inside the library once people started disappearing. They were so easily frightened. Some were even spooked by the Pressmen on the square with their strange green stone.

So Xachar had gone alone, leaving his group on the square.

"Good for nothing, wet behind the ears, easily distracted, all of you," he muttered. "You'll stay in the Far Reaches." He'd proven he was better.

At home, in the Riverward Kingdom, Xachar hadn't been considered useful either. Sure, he'd been good with the farm equipment, but his aunt and uncle had been better. He'd passed his first engineering tests, but others had scored higher. He'd disliked both farming and engineering—had wanted to try something beyond his family farm. But that took learning, and books, and there weren't any at home that weren't practical or relevant to farming and tools.

Universities had such books, Xachar knew. But there was no money for university.

During the spring rains, his work boots had squelched in the thick mud of the farm, echoing his thoughts: *Stuck here, stuck here.* In the summer, his rough cotton shirt clung damply to his neck as he helped with the weeding among the vegetables. *Stuck, stuck, stuck*, said the weeds. In the fall, as they harvested and then sold their food for not enough money beyond a season's supplies and equipment repairs, Xachar's skin itched with the sameness of it all.

Still, his frustration didn't make him angry. It made him slow and sad. Even when he slept, his dreams were about walking the same fields his parents had walked. Repeatedly. *Slow, stuck, stuck.*

Now he knew he was too stuck in reality too. Too slow to even chase a librarian out of hiding. Xachar shook his head. No one else knew that yet, though. He still had a chance.

When the Pressmen had come to his village, they'd held a small parade. Few had paid attention, but Xachar had gone. He'd taken a pamphlet from one of the blue-uniformed marchers. "We're sharing knowledge, for everyone," she'd explained. "It's important."

Xachar's mouth hung open. "I feel the same way." She'd been beautiful, that marcher. But her words had been even prettier.

He'd read their pamphlets. He'd listened when another speaker described the Pressmen's dream. "Everyone," they said, "should be able to learn whatever they want. Whenever they want."

This, Xachar realized, was his calling. To make such a thing possible. If not for himself, for others. So no one would be stuck.

At the end of the parade, when the Pressmen asked him to help, Xachar decided to be useful. A pen was placed in his hand. A piece of paper, with *Knowledge for Everyone* at the top, was set before him, and the ink had run green on the page, his signature a ribbon, tying him to them. Indelible. Flowing. He'd sighed happily.

The Pressmen gave him a book-shaped pin in exchange for his name. To his surprise, a year later, they'd asked him to go to the Far Reaches, to school. They'd help pay if Xachar agreed to bring them the deeds to his family's farm equipment as a sign he was serious.

Once at Far Reaches University, Xachar hadn't made a great student, either, in those long months before the Pressmen appeared. But that was according to plan. He'd been ready, with enough others who understood the Pressmen's philosophy to help the university's transition. The Pressmen had been glad for the information he'd sent back, the books he'd given them with promises of more. He became what he'd dreamed, but this time for the greater good.

~

Still, Xachar had to admit to himself now that he was a terrible judge of academics. He'd thought once the Pressmen used their technology to start sinking the buildings, everyone would run away. Instead, the academics who remained stubbornly ran *toward* the buildings. Which had made catching them difficult.

His failures had compounded, overrunning his successes, each feeling worse than the last. No Pressmen wanted any part of failure. He'd already noticed others in the dorm leaving him alone more.

But while he'd been a student, Xachar had read several adventure novels in the library. He knew now that he only needed one good chance, and everything could turn right around.

When he'd spotted the thief skulking among the fallen buildings, he followed her. He staged an accident—well, he tried, then he actually did get trapped.

His panic had been real enough that it got the thief to rescue him, and to his surprise, she gave him her books and went back for more.

Tricking the thief was a perfect opportunity. Xachar found his squad leader. This was his chance. He convinced her to send in more Pressmen and dogs.

"Too many good people have disappeared in that library," she said. "We were going to wait. You'd best be right."

They'd given chase. They'd been so close. And then—both the librarian, wanted for questioning in the disappearance of those Pressmen, *and* the thief disappeared.

At least they'd left the books behind.

But it wasn't enough. The look on the captain's face was obvious.

"We'll find you," she said, "something suitable."

Xachar swallowed. His chances for a future with the

Pressmen were narrowing. The ribbon of his name on the paper beneath *Knowledge for Everyone,* fading. The university was closing, the farm not an option anymore. And now he was being assigned "something suitable" by the Pressmen. Xachar's breath ran ragged with worry.

He knew what "suitable" meant. He'd had letters from home in the months since the parades in the Riverward.

Since then both his uncle and aunt, the best machinery engineers the farm had, had gone with the Pressmen to Quadril. "The Pressmen made a fuss about your uncle," his mother wrote. "Your aunt hissed at him. Pulled him back. Told him to fetch the cows. But finally they were persuaded to go."

And then the Pressmen came back for his parents too. A neighbor wrote to tell Xachar, the letter arriving the day of the Last Meeting. "They were found suitable jobs."

It is a long struggle, Xachar thought. *If this is the price for everyone being able to learn whatever they want, whenever they want it, this sacrifice is worth it.*

As long as he could help. As long as he could be useful, not just suitable.

Being useful was his chance to control his future, Xachar knew this in his heart. Applying for a position in Quadril, rather than being taken away somewhere and given a "suitable" job, seemed an easier fate. Better reputation—like his uncle. Perhaps he could find his family.

It dawned on him: *They had a drain on people with machine skills.*

"Wait." Xachar followed the captain. "I'm good with tools. I'm quick. I can help you."

"What kind of tools?" the captain said.

"Farm machinery, mostly," Xachar muttered. "Engineering." The life he'd tried to get away from. Was it enough?

The captain nodded. "You can escort the shipment of books back to Quadril and see if someone there will find you more training. I hear they have some trouble with the press now and then." By the sound of her voice, she seemed to think this was a perfect solution for Xachar. "But don't fail this time, young man. It's your last chance."

Within hours, he was on a boat to Quadril. He wouldn't fail. Xachar promised himself he wouldn't become stuck this time.

~

The Pressmen's boats had motors, not sails. Coal-fed ironclads. Their shadows clipped the waves while dark clouds curled out of their smokestacks and tinted the sky.

Xachar threw up the entire journey, but learned to stay to the leeward side, finally.

When he stumbled off the boat, they took him to a small room and read the letter the captain had sent along with him.

He'd known he was a terrible guard—and the captain's letter made it clear she thought he was terrible at everything. But he hadn't lied. He was good with tools. Old tools especially. And the Pressmen, once they realized he hated closed spaces, chuckled. "We have the perfect job for you. Not that you'll remember. None of you remember."

What a strange thing to say. But the Pressmen took him through rows of tents and long barracks to a central brick building and a man called the Presskeeper. The Presskeeper clapped Xachar on the shoulder and led him down a long hall. "Glad to have a volunteer again. Welcome to the Great Press. Until you receive further training, all you need to do is feed it books, understand?"

Xachar nodded. He wouldn't fail.

The press's outer room had been terrifying.

A group of four Pressmen with close-cropped hair sat doing simple tasks. Feeding newly blank books into a slim, high-tech press. Dumping sacks of strange ink—dust, really—across the pages within a glass and iron box. The dust swirled like a storm. Then books emerged, filled *Uni-*

versal Compendiums of Knowledge. The Presskeeper lifted a still-warm book for him to see: *Far Reaches University*, the entry read. *Two hundred years and counting, raising leaders in a region known for shipping and fishing.*

As Xachar watched, the letters tangled and blurred, a ribbon of ink curling in on itself and releasing. When it stopped, the page read *Two hundred years of knowledge hoarding in a region known for shipping and fishing.*

The Presskeeper gently closed the book and passed it back to a worker at the press. She smiled blankly at him.

With a jolt, Xachar recognized the woman. He whispered, "Aunt Nessa?" She looked pale and distracted. Not the feisty woman he remembered.

The Presskeeper walked toward the inner room as Xachar tried to speak to his aunt. To ask where the rest of his family were. But she stared at him as if she didn't know him.

Xachar stuffed the fear in his throat down so he wouldn't cry out. The Presskeeper opened the door to the inner room, and Xachar bit his lip. He would not think of his parents, or of the others he'd left behind at the university. Of the professors on the square.

No. He had to keep moving forward.

The Pressman standing next to his aunt wiped his face with a damp sleeve, careful not to sweat on the *Compendiums* that slid off the press, ready to be bound.

"What happened to them?" Xachar finally whispered. He didn't indicate he knew any of them. Safer that way. He felt his heart rewriting itself, like the words in the book.

"Their minds got wiped clean. All that knowledge, and they're stacking books. Five of them so far," the head of the press said without smiling. "You'll be the sixth. Lucky number, right? Like the number of old kingdoms, before the Jeweled Valley fell. Maybe you'll last."

Xachar stopped in his tracks. The Presskeeper's hand was on the door to the inner room. "Last?"

"You'll be fine," the man said, holding the thick, dark oak door half open for him. His blue and white uniform stood out cleanly in the drab greenish light. He didn't enter the room.

Xachar watched him for a moment.

"Just keep it fed, and it won't hurt you," the Presskeeper said, laughing a little before letting the door go. It swung shut with a long squeak.

Xachar put his hand up to stop the door and looked out the gap, into the bigger room. The Presskeeper's broad frame didn't disappear between one moment and the next like the two academics in the library had. He retreated with normal footfalls, then turned a corner, even as his words echoed in Xachar's ears.

~

Hours later, in the close, noisy room lit with dark green light the color of late-night shadows, Xachar battled claustrophobia again. His eyes throbbed; he could taste the dark ink on the back of his teeth. The walls drew close around him. The press breathed hot, inky gusts as it thunked and thudded its way through the Far Reaches library.

Just keep it fed.

He had six hours left on his first lonely press-feeding shift. He wouldn't fail. He took a deep breath and kept working, ignoring the panic that tugged at him.

His hands ached from splitting the spines of books brought back from the Far Reaches and feeding them facedown through the press wheels. Each time the lathes turned over and the latest book came through, eviscerated and emptied of ink, Xachar felt the room grow smaller, his shirt grow damp with sweat.

But he didn't leave.

He focused on the press.

It seemed very old, but modifications had been made. A thick metal frame held the intake rollers—once a cylinder that guided paper over a typesetting roller—that worked in tandem to suck whole books in and crush them. A drip hose kept the pages from getting too hot as the press moved faster, and rusting trays on each side gathered ink that was pressed out. The resulting machine looked a lot like farm equipment, but a little less sharp.

Farm equipment required power, usually steam or coal. Xachar could find no scuttle, no fire. Instead, the press seemed to run on its own. He shivered.

Keep it fed, and it won't hurt you.

Xachar ran a hand across the gears and press levers. The warm metal thickened the smell of ink and pulp in the air. He breathed through his mouth, fighting nausea.

The press thunked and swung; it sang a little as the gears whined. Xachar looked closer. On the farm, they'd worried about gears snapping teeth, especially on large jobs. He'd fed the press a *Hundred-Year History* of something. Then a *Guidelines for Knowledge Sharing* right after. Those had been thick books.

"What's wrong?" he whispered. He wished he had a manual for the machine. The press made a strange sound, like a whisper or a song.

Then, with a loud clunk and a terrible grinding sound, the press stopped entirely. *Stuck!* Xachar's breakfast weighed heavy in his stomach. The room went dead silent. The walls drew ever closer.

How could he keep the press fed if it was broken? Xachar began to sweat in earnest. Salt stung his brow and cracked lips as he gritted his teeth through the final hours of his service, trying to get the press started again.

He picked up the heavy metal toolbox resting by the door and carried it to the main cylinder.

"How can I fix you?" He wasn't supposed to fix anything. *Just keep feeding the machine.* Xachar knew he should call a Pressman, but that would be a failure too. A difficult machine indeed.

Then he saw it, a broken lever grinding against the lower cylinder, a chunk of book jammed far within the mechanism. Xachar was gangly for his age, and fish-belly pale. In the strange pressroom light, he looked forest-green. But as he crawled beneath the pressworks, the heavy metal frame close overhead, he felt strong. Useful.

Gingerly, he worked the pages from the machine, tearing a few, retrieving a half-erased portrait of an unknown man from the gears. A few more pages. He nudged the broken part out of the cylinder's path. A coil of metal.

Xachar looked for a replacement piece, without finding one. He would have to call for help. He didn't want to yet. Beneath the press, he spread the crumpled pages he'd rescued before him, half erased.

Guidelines for single-source sharing of resources across the Western Mountains, the pages still said, though the following pages were mostly blank. The text was from early in the knowledge struggles, when a small group from the Western Mountains demanded that the Six Kingdoms synchronize their records. That hadn't gone well, Xachar remembered from his library class with the Master Archivist.

The libraries had protested by tearing Western Mountains manuals up and distributing them evenly across their regions. The crinkled evidence of that rebellion—a document from the Western Mountains that had come to rest in the Far Reaches—lay in his hands.

That was about the time of the parade that had come to the Riverward.

When Pressmen's groups had grown and prospered in various cities. Held parades and large, raucous meetings in libraries. The Pressmen's ideals, merged with the strength of the Western Mountains, seemed to become something entirely more powerful than either one apart.

Xachar freed the last of the guidelines from the press and patted the cylinders.

The press stopped making horrible clunking noises, but the cylinders didn't roll again. Still, Xachar felt his spirits lift. He'd fixed something!

Perhaps he would be more than useful here. If he could get the press running again.

Xachar looked closely at the broken lever, avoiding the sharper gears. It was a long one, with one end buried deep in the press's heart, bound by the lathes. No. Xachar shook his head as his eyes adjusted further to the shadows beneath the press. He'd been mistaken: the piece was a piston, not a lever. Without a source of steam, a piston made no sense, but there it was. Plain as day. This kept the press rolling.

He looked deeper, trying to find a power source.

Above the piston, Xachar saw a complex shape, unlike any of the press's other braces or gears. A green sphere, thick with facets. Hissing slightly.

Each facet caught the room's greenish dazzle.

Xachar whistled. At the center of the press was a good-sized gem, the same color as the stones the Pressmen had in the Far Reaches. But this was much larger. And secret. Invisible to the outside. Glowing darkly green in the room's light.

No. That was wrong too. The pressroom was glowing green because of the gem.

As Xachar continued to look over the stilled machinery and throughout the room, hoping to find a replacement coil for the piston, the gem's dark tones faded.

He finally found the part deep in the toolbox. But when he turned back to the press, color had drained from the gem until it was a pale shadow of itself. By the time he replaced the compression coil, the emerald seemed smaller too, the room dark.

Xachar's shift was almost over.

The door slammed out of its frame and hit the wall. "Your output is low, Xachar. The outer room needs more blank books!"

The Presskeeper seemed more worried than angry. When he saw Xachar beneath the press, he blinked, then growled, "Get out of there."

"I'm almost finished fixing it," Xachar said. "There was a jam."

The Presskeeper grabbed Xachar's foot and pulled. Xachar slid across the ink-slick floor as the man muttered, "You . . . fixed the press? You should have alerted me."

"But I thought I could fix it," Xachar said. "And I did." He waited for praise. He'd been very useful.

The Presskeeper seemed to grow as he returned to lean against the door. "You need to learn about the proper way to do things, including how not to damage expensive machinery. Or yourself." He huffed and swore. Then, finally, he leaned against the door frame. "Tell me what you did to my press."

From the floor, Xachar described the fix.

"You said you were good with tools. I say you were lucky. Good men have been lost trying to fix this press. Getting too close to the"—the Presskeeper gestured at where the gem rested, hidden now—"has consequences."

"It just felt like what I was doing was right," Xachar said.

"Just felt like . . . ," the Presskeeper sputtered. "This press, and its workings, are known to only a few, young man." He closed the door and stood before it, hands forming fists at his hips. "If you've been sent from another Pressman faction to spy on the Midnight Emerald, you will not make it out of here."

"No! I crawled into the workings and fixed the jam, then stayed to fix the piston," Xachar answered, feeling a little breathless now at the thought. Something about what the Presskeeper was saying nagged at the back of his mind. He began to sweat again. "I'm no spy! I was told to keep the press fed! That's all I wanted to do!" His voice cracked with panic.

"You've seen a state secret," the Presskeeper said. "You have two choices. Work here, sleep close by, speaking to no one outside the barracks. Or . . ."

"Or?"

"We're at a sort of war, young man. There are spies in war. I thought we were safe because so few can get as close to the Midnight Emerald as you did, and fewer still could leave this building afterward." The Presskeeper frowned. "But you're not drooling or shouting about visions. We are tasked with a very important responsibility here. Knowledge for everyone. And anyone who turns against us is committing treason."

Treason? Xachar wondered. Against Knowledge? But he bit his tongue. Agreed to stay with the press, its greenish light, its strange noises.

"Then I'll try you out as my assistant Presskeeper. You will fix it when it breaks and clear all jams. You'll keep the press fed, both manuscripts and ink." He said it with the sort of relief in his voice Xachar had heard from his parents when he'd gotten old enough to mind the cows. "Though no one's lasted long enough yet to be useful."

Xachar was useful.

"What ink does the press require?" Xachar began. He felt a strange mix of triumph—he had a job, he hadn't failed—and fear—he wasn't sure he wanted this particular job. In order to do it, he'd have to keep information from others. Which wasn't what he'd wanted at the parade so long ago. *Knowledge for Everyone.* That was important.

But sometimes, to achieve a goal, compromises must be made. Xachar knew this. The Pressmen pairing with the Western Mountains, for one.

"The ink from the manuscripts deepens the emerald's power, which keeps the press running. The dust from the press has certain properties. . . . Sit down."

Xachar sat.

"The old gems of the Jeweled Valley. Heard of them?" the Presskeeper began. "They did spectacular things. Hid a whole kingdom from armies for centuries. Destroyed minds. Dangerous things. All of them gone now. But the emerald inside the press is sort of like that. As long as it has ink and paper to keep running."

"And what did you do when it broke before I got here?" He had to ask.

The Presskeeper jerked his head toward the hall. "I'd drag the latest operator from the room and fix it myself."

And the Presskeeper then began to speak of things so strange that Xachar could only nod. It would be many days before he truly understood, and by then he would know more than the Presskeeper did.

5.

Jorit

Between one moment and the next, Jorit was torn from the sunken library's dusty confines and dropped unceremoniously on the forest floor, Ania beside her.

The Far Reaches' ocean breezes were gone. The gulls, silent; the seashell-riddled crunch of the paving stones outside the library, exchanged for mud.

How?

Pine tar, burning. The bitter smell of a fired cannon. Jorit coughed, pawing through a haze of smoke, and in the near distance, she spotted a palace built in an ancient style, in flames. No refuge there.

For a moment she wondered what wealth lay inside such a palace, and whether it would be worth looking. But the clock still ticked against her hand and called her to reason. Ania clung to the device too.

A river glinted between evergreen trunks. Sparks against dark shadows, instead of the Far Reaches' lowland moonlight silvering the archipelago's edges.

Where are we? "What happened?" Jorit whispered, and started to crawl away, trying to stay low.

Eyes squeezed shut, Ania cried out in fear and grabbed for her, nearly dropping the timepiece. "Don't! Don't let go."

Jorit bent toward her, the panic in her voice too much to ignore. The air whistled as a stone was heaved from the castle wall. The projectile flew right over their heads.

"You don't let go, I won't let go," Ania whispered. Her voice had an odd lilt to it.

Jorit held tight to both Ania and the timepiece. "I won't," she promised. Ania was shaking violently. So was Jorit.

"We're in danger here too!" Ania whispered, even as Jorit wondered where "here" was.

"Not the Far Reaches. Not anywhere near . . . " she said. "How do we find a safe place to go?"

They had to get away from falling rocks and fires. Away from attacking guards wearing ancient Western Mountains insignia.

Ancient Western Mountains . . . Jorit gasped again, breathed in smoke, and doubled over in another coughing fit. "We're in the valley."

Another look around once she stopped coughing, and she was certain. This was the valley of her great-grandmothers' childhood. Maybe earlier. By the time Jorit was born, before her family fled, there'd been many fewer trees. Still, she'd know the woods and the river anywhere, and the ruins, somewhat.

But evergreens weren't the right trees—and the ruins . . . weren't ruins. Jorit's limbs grew heavy with panic.

A young woman ran past them, dressed in a tunic that Jorit could only think of as *archaic*. Her hair was snarled in knots, and her face streaked with tears. She didn't look left or right, just dashed for the river, heedless of Ania's soft whimper at the sight of her.

"It's not safe!" Ania said again, more out of shock than fear. She started to pull away but still clung to the timepiece. Jorit refused to let go of it either. A worry tickled her. The clock. The cloud. The ancient castle.

The clock began to tick faster.

"The disappeared Pressmen. The Master Archivist," Ania whispered again, her eyes wide. "You sent them here?" She looked around, as if for a lost friend. The clock gears grated loudly. "No. Not here. Too early."

"Who are you talking to?" Jorit wheeled on her companion. "You did this to us?"

"I don't think so?" Ania said. "I—" Her eyes widened. Jorit looked over her shoulder. More soldiers came from the palace.

"Answer me!" Jorit pulled the librarian and the clock

behind a large stone formation. Ania resisted the whole way as the clock grew heavier in their hands. "Or help get us out of here."

"I don't know how!"

Jorit considered the clock—their only weapon—and whether she could use it against a soldier. She thought for a moment about leaving Ania to them while she escaped. But when she looked at the older woman, her braid disheveled, confusion overtaking fear in her brown-flecked eyes, and the clock both of them held tight to, Jorit knew she couldn't do it. The librarian had helped her—a thief. She would help the librarian.

She hissed in pain as the clock case heated up. The beat of the clock escalated until it again crescendoed, and Jorit's heart kept time with it.

"We have to keep the clock safe," Ania said. "It's our only way home."

Jorit scoffed. "It's a broken timepiece with a cooling problem." But she knew it was more. She'd seen the glow. Had felt the heat. Even if the grating and ticking didn't sound like anything but an old clock.

In the shade of their hiding place, Ania's eyes rolled back into her head, and Jorit grabbed her before she fell. She lowered her unwished-for companion to the soot-marred grass while sparks dropped all around them.

"The soldiers, the valley's fall, the Jewel," Ania whispered. "Everything begins. Everything ends. I'll save what I can."

Then, as before, the ticks seemed to stretch out.

Hair prickled on the back of Jorit's neck. Her arms sprung up goose bumps. "Teach me not to steal from a library," she whispered, not letting go of the clock or the librarian. For once, the thing Jorit knew best was that she was afraid.

But it wasn't the clock that frightened her. Ania had said "the valley's fall." The Sixth Kingdom—they were watching it end. And if they weren't careful, Jorit realized, they might disappear with it.

Ania's murmurs grew softer. Then paused as if someone answered. Jorit strained her ears, but all she heard was cries for help from the distant palace.

Another figure ran toward the river, dragging a cloak filled with shards of leaded crystal. In the firelight, the green fabric looked as if it were bleaching white. The glass looked black and green, the color of the Pressmen's gems.

The clock ticks became one long sound, and the world drew gray and close again. Jorit could hear her heartbeat in her ears. Her breath stretched out painfully, as if she were being pulled along a thread, becoming the thread; it was sickening, almost maddening. She held on tight to Ania. To anything familiar as she watched the clock.

The timepiece's hands spun backward. The bezel

points seemed to all glow at once, even as the ticks became one long noise and the world faded around them.

When Jorit came to, Ania was gone, and the timepiece too.

~

She lay beside an alley-shadowed puddle, the sewer stink wretched all around. Between the gap of buildings, sounds of a parade echoed. A flash of blue and white fabric appeared. Had Western Mountains armies found her valley hiding spot?

No, Jorit wasn't in the valley. The building wall bore a sign for a restaurant in East Quadril. One Jorit's grandparents had often remembered fondly. The sign was new.

Jorit got to her feet. There were no marching soldiers here either. The street was filled with banners that said *Share Knowledge*. Men and women wore blue and white sashes, carried freshly written placards.

Pressmen.

But different ones than Jorit knew. These Pressmen smiled and waved, and there weren't that many of them. The parade barely stretched three blocks. Few of the marchers wore the familiar blue and white, just pins and patches with a book on them, mostly handmade. People on the street cheered as the Pressmen handed out leaflets. Two men carried a trestle of pale green gems in the parade's midst. A banner on the trestle read *Knowledge: More Valuable Than Gems.*

Jorit squinted. She could make out glass gems—certainly fakes, discernable even from a distance. What were the Pressmen up to?

As she watched, a Pressman stepped away from the parade to relieve himself against the alley wall. When he spotted her, he stepped quickly back out into the street with a swish of rough cotton workman's clothes.

Ania appeared around the corner and pulled Jorit away from the parade. "You're awake!"

"Where are we?"

"In Quadril," she said, and hesitated. "I think. But this march happened decades ago. My mother watched it from her parents' window, until her grandmother caught her and pulled her away. She called it the Parade of the Last Gems and the First Knowledge."

Jorit knew the name. "You're from Quadril?" She almost said "also" but bit her tongue.

Ania shook her head. "My family is. I was born in the Far Reaches. But they're here. Somewhere close. Why are we here?"

Jorit frowned. "Our ancestors were neighbors, then." But she knew they hadn't been. Her family was from the valley. No one took you seriously if you said you were from the valley—so much bad luck there. So many strange things had happened there. Once, the Pressmen had been interested in things like that. They'd offered a high price for information about the valley and its gems to the nearby mining school. She and Marton had gotten in trouble for refusing. Now Jorit didn't want that kind of attention ever again.

If her family had been scholars like Ania's, Jorit would have been able to attend the mining school without a problem, instead of struggling to gather the fees. But they also would have been driven out when the Pressmen really took hold. The universities in Quadril were the first to close.

Instead, the hum of giant machinery printing the day's news and readings had been one of Jorit's earliest memories, and joys. Before. But that was in the future. Now the Pressmen were only a parade.

"Your family left after the first marches. Mine stayed." Jorit waved her hand. She felt the air move against her skin. Heard the cries from the marchers. Smelled the roast nuts the street hawkers had rushed to bring out once they saw the parade coming.

She was here and now. She didn't believe it. Wouldn't believe it.

These Pressmen were so different from the ones who sacked universities. They were friendly. From the looks of their outfits and the gem display, not altogether well unified yet either.

Ania nodded. "I can prove it." She held out a fresh leaflet. This one was printed roughly on grasspaper, in an old style. No. Jorit looked closer; it was machine set, the letter forms rough and hand-pressed. A very new art, for the time.

"Printed."

Ania nodded, taking the paper back. *More knowledge is better. Learn how to spot accuracy.* "I remember Grandmother talking about this march," she said. "Everyone thought the Pressmen seemed smart." She shuddered. "That they'd add to the local arts and culture, not—"

"Control it?" Jorit nodded. "Something changed."

The alley grew lighter as the sun rose high in the sky. The street began to steam. More smells: horses, sweat.

More shouts, this time from the street. Men and women wearing academic robes marking them as members of the two nearest local universities yelled. Their arms swung and their robes belled out as they threw fruit. In an instant, a Pressman's white cotton shirt turned brown and streaked with tomato seeds. Jorit smelled rot.

"You cannot use what you can't understand; knowledge refined is better than knowledge to hand!" More academics shouted the Pressmen down. The crowd seemed to stutter, its affections pulled both ways.

The Pressmen still smiled, but their parade slowed. "We differ in our opinions, that is all," one of the bearers of the false gems said.

"You are wrong! That is worse!" a professor shouted. "You need education, not just knowledge. Progress cannot happen without refinement. Discourse."

"But you would choose who gets to talk. Who progresses."

Both sides now were stilled in the street; the fruit had transformed into fists.

Nausea rose in Jorit's throat. Her grandmother had never mentioned there was an altercation. No one was right here.

Leaflets scattered on the ground as small brawls began to knot the parade. Jorit pulled Ania's arm, but the librarian stared across the street. "Did you see that woman?"

A young Pressman fell to the ground. Her companions carried her to the sidewalk.

"What?" Jorit looked. "Who?"

"Handing out flyers. Gone now," Ania said. "She looked so familiar."

Jorit peered toward the street and the parade, but dragged her friend back into the shadows as another Pressman took shelter in the alley, with two friends, calling, "Come out, friends, and help us."

You're not our friends, Jorit thought, pulling Ania

against the wall. *And we must not be pulled into this.* But it was too late. Sunlight shadowed the Pressmen's faces and shoulders, their fruit-stained placards blocking more of the sun as they stepped between the buildings.

Fear can slow things down, same as sorrow, she knew. But even as time seemed to still, she saw that they were trapped.

Another dead end.

"How did we escape before?" Jorit whispered. "Now would be a good time to do it again. It's not safe here either."

The sounds of fighting faded, then belled again as the few remaining Pressmen dropped their placards and ran for cover. The alley-bound Pressmen sighed and ducked deeper into the shadows for cover too. They didn't ask for Ania and Jorit's help again.

Ania stared at the clock in her hands. "I wish I knew." Fear tightened her voice around each word. As she spoke, the timepiece began to tick faster.

A new time wasn't necessarily better, Jorit realized. The clock's one setting seemed to be danger. *Will we ever see home again?* she wondered. Not necessarily the where, but the when.

"Not back to the library, but to our own time? Perhaps?" *Yes.* She wanted to live in that time, or at least live past it. Jorit couldn't keep the urgency out of her voice.

"I don't know how," Ania said. She stared at the clock case, which was growing hotter. Glowing, in fact. "All right," she said.

"Who are you talking to?" Jorit wanted to shake her.

One lone Pressman walked into the street. He held a piece of lead glass. Raised it to catch the sun and refract it into the shadows. Green-tinted light angled toward them.

Then the flyer Ania held began to lose its color. And the glass? The prism turned the gray-green color of the page's ink.

Ania crumpled the flyer into her pocket as the prism turned dark as midnight. Instead of glass, the Pressman now held what looked like an emerald, much like the gems on the trencher, but far darker.

He turned it toward the academics. Meantime, the other Pressmen came after the librarian and the thief, even as more Pressmen advanced on the scholars.

Jorit pressed Ania as far back in the alley as she could, climbing a pile of trash that was pushed against the wall, trying to get higher, to buy more time, to become part of the scenery.

This time, there was no clockroom to hide in, no way to disappear. "Come on, clock!"

Ania whimpered as a Pressman grabbed roughly at her boot. She stumbled on the garbage pile but did not drop the clock or the flyer. The inside of the paper still had ink on it.

Jorit pulled Ania upright again and then clasped her companion's arm. The clock's ticking grew loud and insistent until the minutes blended together. The world swung around their heads.

Once more, they were pulled through the sound. Jorit and Ania hung on to each other, no longer strangers, or enemies.

TESTIMONY OF THIEF JORIT LEE
BEFORE THE COMMISSION ON
KNOWLEDGE AND LOYALTY
INTERIM REPORT

In the continuing excerpt, the commission notes that Jorit Lee has no affiliations, none to recommend her, aside from the librarian. She is marked as a thief. We are not convinced of her loyalties, and in the aftermath of this turbulent time, such things are most important.

Commissioner Novil (leaning toward the thief): While no one makes paper this way any longer, there is no aging or damage. Your sample is nearly blank with only a few faded ink marks on it. All illegible. This seems the greatest of conveniences. It is obviously a fake.

Commissioner Andol: Do you expect this committee to accept this as evidence of your travels? Or did you steal it from a library during more recent events?

The question hangs in the air above the subject before Commissioner Novil continues.

Commissioner Novil: We've all seen the mark on your hand, madam.

The thief does not answer.

Commissioner Andol: Your silence will be taken as guilt.

Jorit Lee shares with the commission a small smile that doesn't reach her eyes. Finally, she speaks.

Jorit Lee: That flyer was freely given.

Commissioner Novil (sputtering): Your concision feels like a challenge. Where, then, is your time traveling machine? What did you change in the past?

Jorit Lee: We cannot change what's already happened, only what will. To attempt otherwise is a trap.

The thief runs her marked hand through her uneven hair. She crosses her arms.

Commissioner Novil: What proof do you have, then, that you did what you claim?

This time, her smile reaches her eyes.

Jorit Lee: My proof is you and I having this conversation.

Commissioner's note: Jorit Lee and her brother were caught stealing books from the East Quadril Mining School in order to pay for their classes. That the brother did not survive the conflicts while Jorit Lee did puts added suspicion on her.

6.

Jorit

When the clock's ticking quieted, Jorit and Ania found themselves standing near a different kind of crowd. Spices and cooking smells filled the air. Jorit heard cries of "Fruit!" and "Finest cloth!"

A news crier's hazel eyes were fixed wide upon them, or upon the space that had been empty until now. The young boy blinked and shook his head before returning to beating the small wood and hide drum he carried and reciting the news he'd been paid to share. "Quadril officially absorbs the valley as a protectorate! The Six Kingdoms are Five!"

The boy still stared at them as he shouted. They stepped away from the transfixed crier, farther into the market, keeping their eyes out for anyone following them.

The valley, its own kingdom, imagine. Jorit focused on staying with Ania through the crowds.

A banner flapping overhead, fringe flying in the wind, wished shoppers a happy new year, but the date made no sense. "This is long *before* my grandmother was born," Ania whispered. "We're going backward."

Jorit had no answer. She kept her grip on her companion, and on the clock. The feeling of waking up in a strange time, alone, was slowly receding.

Or they were growing used to people disappearing. Jorit blinked once, clearing her eyes.

"Look!" Ania pointed to her right. "More timepieces!"

The crowd flowed around them, revealing a long stall glittering with brass and glass. On the near table, pocket watches and familiar looking clocks in wooden cases gleamed, new and shining. The timepiece in their hands looked similar, although far more tarnished and banged up.

Jorit lifted their clock to the light to look closer. Sun caught the glass and dazzled light across her hand, and across the thief's mark. She pulled her hand back to her side, but it was too late.

A sudden commotion behind the stall. Ania turned away, trying to see whether the news crier had pointed them out.

"Thieves!" came a cry close behind her. "My precious timepieces! Thieves!" A strong, scarred hand grabbed her arm.

The shopkeeper bustled Jorit around the stall's front, pointing finger extended right at her head.

Out of the fire, into the cook pan, Jorit thought.

The crowd began to turn, and Jorit's shoulders tensed. But Ania kept her wits. She raised her voice so that nearby shoppers could hear. "Not at all, sir! We came to see if you could repair this antique. It's seen some hard times since our grandmother purchased it!"

The shopkeeper narrowed his eyes. He took in the sight of the aged timepiece with increasing surprise. Some people in the crowd did as well. The shopkeeper stammered, "But this is very similar to one of my original designs! How old did you say it was?"

"It's hard to tell." Jorit recovered herself enough to answer. "Our grandmother herself did not know."

"You claim this truth, and yet you have been marked for stealing." The shopkeeper continued pointing, his thick brows furrowing. Some in the crowd murmured. Pressed closer to see what was happening. "The symbol is clear."

But the crime hadn't been. Jorit frowned. It didn't matter now. The symbol declared her a thief, so she had become one.

But Ania put her hand over Jorit's. "I am no thief. I am a teacher, and I vouch for my cousin. Do you doubt me also?" She lifted her chin and waited for the shopkeeper's verdict.

Jorit tried not to stare at Ania as something like hope fluttered in her throat. She coughed to clear it. Then worried. Were academics respected in this era?

The man frowned at them for a moment, then shook

his head and spoke loud enough for the crowd to hear. "My apologies. I can see that you are an honorable person trying to redeem someone. By your words, a scholar as well."

But he pulled Jorit close, his grip tightening around her elbow. "I doubt you know much about that timepiece. I will find you and this clock when the market closes for lunch. Be nearby. Make yourselves unobtrusive until then."

He bowed to Ania and released Jorit's arm. Gently nudged both of them into the flow of the crowd.

Jorit, still shaken, wondered, *Did they want to be found?*

"He knows the clocks. And the clock knows him. He might tell us how to make it work," Ania murmured, as if answering her thoughts. "It's worth the risk."

They let themselves be moved away, but Jorit bristled. "How do you know?"

Ania didn't answer.

"We have no money, no clothes that aren't vastly out of—or, not yet in—style." She knew how to be unobtrusive. And yet she and Ania, here? "We have no chance of *not* standing out."

The clock ticked loudly on the street's quieter side. Ania seemed to nod at it. "Shhh," she said.

Jorit's stomach growled. That, too, made her cross. "What do you hear when you do that?"

Ania blushed. "Just a memory of an old friend. Nothing more."

Jorit's frown deepened. "Seeing familiar faces in the past, talking to memories?" She didn't like traveling with companions who heard voices. But there were no guards chasing them. And Ania had stood up for her in the square. That was at least something.

Jorit caught sight of exactly what they needed at the market's edge: an inn with a tea shop attached. A shaded table outside, with chairs and a hand-lettered sign offering samples of different teas. The proprietor allowed them to sit once they said they were meeting the shopkeeper, but they had no money for drinks. The smell of spiced tea and honey was distracting. "If we could sell something," Jorit groaned, "we could . . ." But at Ania's sharp look she felt ashamed. "I said *if*. I'm hungry."

"I am too," Ania said, squeezing Jorit's hand. "We'll find a way. Perhaps we can wash dishes in exchange for supper here, once we know more. We know when we are, thanks to the banner and the news crier. Judging by the wares for sale and spices available, we know roughly where—Eastern Shores. Now we just need to know about the clock."

Jorit's breath hitched. Marton had been lost in Eastern Shores.

Her brother. His desire to keep out of the Pressmen's

way. His need to make something of himself. Of them. Lost forever. But not yet. Far in the future.

She let her breath out slowly through her nose. *Think of the present.* Her stomach rumbled.

She eyed a half-eaten biscuit abandoned at the next table. Slipped it into her sleeve when the innkeeper turned away. Offered some to Ania, but her friend shook her head, so Jorit put the bread in her mouth. The grit matched her mood. How to return to the Far Reaches from here? Or what to do if they for some reason jumped backward again? She had no one to tie her to any particular time or place, but she wanted to be able to choose.

This clock seemed to be making choices for them. *The marketplace was a dead end*, she thought. *The valley as well.* "We need to find a way to get back to our own time. So far, the clock seems to work only when we are afraid."

Ania responded grumpily. "How many times a day would you like to make yourself afraid enough that you jump to another century?"

How does a machine know fear? Jorit wondered, still chewing.

"Technically, it's not even times a day. It's every hundred years or so," Ania mused. The corners of her mouth creased, and Jorit's spirits lifted a little.

"The speed of a heartbeat," Jorit guessed, after swallowing. "I've heard the clock speed up, it's matching our heartbeats as we panic. Maybe that winds it up into action? Should we fool ourselves into believing it's not safe here and see where the timepiece takes us?"

"But it *is* safe here. *We'd* know we were lying. It might not work." Ania put her palm on the clock casing. "We could stay in this time. The books are different, but we could work on saving these. Make copies, maybe."

"It's true, Ania, we have nothing to go back for. The university is lost. Your friend." She paused. "My brother. The Pressmen have rewritten everything. Here, at least, some things still work. There are no Pressmen here, yet."

"But we know that eventually the Pressmen will come to the Eastern Shores. Times will get difficult—at least for some. We know this." Ania stared into her teacup. "And I cannot ignore the fact that I have been blind to something important. Those protests? Certain times are always difficult for someone, aren't they?"

Jorit thought about that. Perhaps there was a future without an economy that did not rely upon scarcity to make things valuable. Perhaps if they went far enough back, or forward . . . She stopped her thought before she saw Marton being carried away again.

"What if we don't get back to the right time? Or we get stuck somewhere?" Jorit paused. "Can we ask to go forward?" She bit her lip. Who would they ask?

"We can try asking the shopkeeper." There was that hesitation again. Ania was keeping something to herself. Her answers were either too quick or just a hitch too slow.

What are you concealing? Jorit began to ask, but pressed her lips together when the shopkeeper approached. He narrowed his eyes at the timepiece. "Hello, there."

"You know the clock." Ania had been right. Jorit was surprised.

He nodded. "I may know it. I made one just like it. Sold it about a month ago. May I look inside for my mark?"

Ania's fingers tightened around the timepiece.

"I won't break it. You can open it yourself if you want. If this is one of mine, there's a latch"—he pointed—"right about there."

Ania sprung the latch. Inside, a strange jewel glittered, red and pink and orange, with three turquoise sparkles. A cabochon.

"An opal?" Jorit remembered her lessons from mining school. A gemstone forged under extreme pressures.

"A fire opal. I was asked to place one like it in my clock. Ah. There's my mark. But this kind of damage? Just how does this happen? Just look at it." He swung his arms wide, dismayed.

Ania looked about to tell the man Just How.

"Why would you put a fire opal inside a timepiece?" Jorit spoke quickly. She tried not to calculate how much this gem was worth, here or at any other time.

"Small gems help the bearings work more smoothly. Smooth operations, better balance. Both mean a timepiece stays more on time than with metal. Most watches have some gem bearings. But few are like this. I had to make adjustments." He showed the two women how the fire opal was hollowed in places to allow the gears to move without friction. How a slice of it had been cut away in the back to seat it in the mechanism.

Ania stared at the gem. "I had no idea." The red-speckled fire opal seemed to glow with its own light. Once again, the clock's ticking seemed to grow louder. Her eyes reflected the glow. "Hello," she whispered.

She tilted her head as if she heard an answer.

"Once, long ago, there were many gems from the Jeweled Valley," the shopkeeper said, looking uncomfortably at Ania, before focusing on Jorit. "Now only a few are left."

"*Were* being the most important word," Jorit countered. *Or will be.* "The days of gems waned when our grandparents were still young." It was a safe statement, no matter the time period, she thought, thinking of the valley palace in flames. She'd prefer all talk of the valley and its gems to cease immediately. Bad luck.

"A machine is a set of rules and constraints," the shopkeeper said. "Just as much of a binding as a bezel. And it's true, many valley gems were cracked or lost, or went bad." The shopkeeper paused, thinking. "And the records of them were lost or hidden away. But if you know where to ask, you can still find one or two. Several were stored in objects—mechanisms—to protect them. The mechanisms—a clock, a printing press, a loom—became their bindings. Each was smuggled out of the Jeweled Valley originally; they remain hidden now in the mechanisms."

Jorit's mouth hung open at the audacity. Even then, gem knowledge was dangerous.

Ania paused in her conversation with the clock. Looked at the shopkeeper. "You bound a gem—something you think is one of the last valley gems—in a machine?"

Jorit drew a breath. "Are you mad?" She'd heard so many stories from her grandparents of badly bound gems. Ania had told her *The Book of Gems* contained many cautions about bad settings.

A book the universities had kept from the public. So not everyone knew the dangers.

The shopkeeper stared at Ania intently. "Are you a lapidary?"

"Me?" Ania laughed. "*I* am a *librarian*. A rumpled one at that." She pressed the side of her satchel, where *The Book of Gems* was tucked within the leather. Jorit understood why. Any family from Quadril or the nearby valley, even from way back, would fight over rumors about someone gone gem-mad. It was an easy way to talk about uncomfortable things, as long as it wasn't your family being talked about.

"You said *lapidary* in the old way." Jorit's skin tingled. She'd heard rumors, passed down for generations, especially from her jeweler grandfather, but no one had actually uttered the word. The closest they'd gotten was "gem-whisperer" and a warding gesture. "Are you one?"

"Oh, no," the shopkeeper said. "I merely dabble. Experiment. This clock was my most successful project, and I had instructions. I was lucky." He blinked quickly, as if grit was stuck in his eye.

"You dabble," Jorit finally countered. "Lapidaries had a trust to wield the old gems because they are dangerous. Dabbling sounds reckless." She frowned. "And the gems. Are the ones you speak of even real? I don't recall any fire opals."

The shopkeeper shrugged, raising an eyebrow. "*Lapidary* is an old word, old habit. There are still some gems in Quadril—little ones, broken pieces. I see them smuggled through the markets now and then. I... experimented. Many are, as you might expect, fakes. Some very good ones." He paused at Jorit's sharp intake of breath. "Usually lead glass, dyed colors—well, my father found one, once, that mimicked every aspect of a valley gem. It whispered. But it could not hold its color. And it drove everyone who touched it into senility or worse. Like they knew nothing and never had." The shopkeeper stared into space. "He had only begun teaching me. I wish we'd had more time."

"Strange," Ania whispered. "How could a fake gem whisper?"

Jorit had heard this lecture at the mining school in Quadril. "The light- and air-bending properties of some gems, some think. Chemicals added in the heating process create channels for an effect like whispering—driving heat and adjusting airflow within the crystal structure to make sounds that only a sensitive few could hear, fewer still interpret as whispers, and a minority could tolerate without losing their minds. Synthetics grow faster too. Are more profitable than gem hunting." The information had quickened her interest in the valley, and triggered her research. She rubbed at her hand.

Ania pursed her lips. "You sound like a professor, not a thief."

Jorit eyed her companion carefully. The librarian had initially seemed so distant, haughty even. And the shopkeeper's disdain still stung. But then words began to tumble from her lips without any sense of self-preservation.

"I'd wanted to be a scholar. But there were no gems left to speak of—or to—anymore. And then the Pressmen came. My studies came to nothing." *Except that the Pressmen branded me and my brother thieves for refusing to help with their projects.* Jorit rubbed her hand.

The shopkeeper stared at her now. "Crystal structure? Chemicals?"

Of course. They were way too early to speak of such things. Jorit stifled a rueful laugh. She'd nearly given them away. "Is the fire opal real?" She asked.

The shopkeeper nodded. "I have no reason to believe it isn't. Though I've never heard it whisper. Have you heard it?" He bent to the clock and began pointing out some of the timepiece's finer details. His ear was close to the gem. He didn't see Ania startle, then take a deep breath and smooth her sleeves with shaking hands.

"You see this extra dial? This is—" He chuckled.

"What?" Jorit held her breath, trying to pay attention to Ania and the shopkeeper both. The man might tell them how to control where the clock went. Ania might reveal what she'd been hiding.

"I'd been asked to construct this timepiece according to a very specific set of standards. Some I thought were completely ridiculous, and I was tempted to stop. A year bezel. A second one, on a free-rotating pin. Another set of amplifying modifications." He ran his fingers along the clock's sides, brushing several flanges.

But while the shopkeeper said much, his hands said more. His fingers lingered on the clock's case. "You aren't from this time, are you?"

Ania froze. "Of course we are. Don't be ridiculous."

His fingers curled around the wood frame. A shocking display from a salesman.

Ania tried to distract him. "Why did you make the timepiece? The other machines? For whom?"

The shopkeeper kept a hand on the clock, but answered. "My father was asked to bind an emerald years ago by a stranger. He didn't know how, but he thought he'd give it a try. I watched him work on the design. Improve it. When a woman came to the shop with this stone and her specifications, I wanted to try too."

"Even though you didn't know how." Jorit's green eyes narrowed. She was starting to suspect. "You're *not* a lapidary."

The shopkeeper shook his head. "I did a lot of guesswork. I'd heard rumors. I got lucky with the clock. A woman from one of the inns nearby had a book about gems with her. Showed me what to do. If only my father had the same."

"Who was the woman?" Ania countered. Her eyes were sharp. "What did she look like?"

But the shopkeeper's fingers had edged over the timepiece again, greedier now. Ania pulled it back, seemingly without thinking.

"Binding is a skill that's worth good money. I'm the only one in Quadril who's tried. I practiced on synthetics until I could make a complex bezel. And I've made many clocks. It seemed natural to try." He was almost murmuring to the clock now.

Jorit frowned. Reached out to the clock.

The man continued, "I did the work when I thought it was a lark. Now that I know? This clock is worth much more than I was paid. It was stolen from me . . . and now you're here. You *are* thieves, but not the usual kind. Tell me how to make it work—"

His fingers became claws as he tried to wrest the timepiece from Ania, who grasped at it too now, fingers slipping.

Jorit pushed the shopkeeper off balance. "You've been paid for this clock. It was not stolen." Her voice rose so the nearby market could hear her. "You cannot demand to be paid a second time." The shopkeeper fell back as several shoppers stared at him and began to whisper.

Taking Ania's arm, Jorit pulled her from her seat. "Come on, Ania." They walked as calmly as they could to the street.

The shopkeeper watched them go. Jorit's heart pounded as they escaped.

7.

Ania

We cannot stay here, Ania thought as they walked into the street. *Not in this now. But we cannot leave yet either. We need to know more.* Her heart was beating faster. Would her panic spirit them away again?

The shopkeeper. He'd bound this gem. Perhaps poorly. *Dabbling.* Ania felt another hitch of alarm. He should have known better than to try.

She'd allowed herself to relax in the tea shop, the beverage's warmth sustaining her after the barrage of the past days.

But this here and now wasn't any safer, neither for her nor for Jorit.

For the clock either, it seemed. Nor was careening from time to time and place to place.

Ania forced herself to breathe. In. Two beats. Out. Two beats. She worked to slow her heart. To keep the clock from taking them away again.

They needed to stay here. For now.

Think, Ania. They'd arrived in the time close to when the clock was created. Close enough to find out about the strange gems. Could they find the press the news crier had mentioned? Was that what the shopkeeper's father had tried to bind?

She and Jorit dodged down a narrower side street, trying to avoid dead-end alleys. Jorit led, pulling Ania along by a sleeve.

Ania skidded to a halt as she remembered something Sonoria Vos had said about a rash of books that went missing in the past. Closer to this now. She remembered her grandmother's stories from Quadril, about opening several favorite books to find them blank. Only a few. Library archives elsewhere had kept copies, but, in the light of future events, those mysterious disappearances made Ania clutch the clock. Had the gem been set in a Pressman's machine?

Had they found the point in time where the Pressmen began?

Could they fix it? Could they save the affected books? Maybe change something?

Behind them, the shopkeeper hadn't pursued them. The two women stopped for breath. The clock's ticking stayed even.

"What if," Ania began, the idea forming in her mind

as she spoke, the words coming out jumbled, "it's not the clock but the fire opal hidden inside the mechanism that's able to skip around in time?" It certainly felt like that was what had happened. "And he mentioned two other mechanisms. A loom and a printing press. What if, instead of being bound and controlled correctly, according to *The Book of Gems*, the mechanisms have magnified their power? In the same way a lever or a pulley lets a person do more work?"

"The *Universal Compendiums of Knowledge* have capacities that the Pressmen won't explain—the words revise and update themselves. No book does that. What if—" Jorit couldn't go on.

Ania knew all the fears that could fill that quiet: *What if there are still more gems? What if they're as dangerous and powerful as the myths? What if the Pressmen really do have one?*

Worse, what if we have another?

"The shopkeeper said his family was asked to set the gems," Jorit panted, staring at the ground. "Who asked him to do it?"

"No," Ania said. "We can't return to the market to ask him. He'll try to take the clock again. He could have us arrested. We need to stay off the street." She pointed to another inn's sign, swinging from a metal pole over a faded green door.

They knocked, and when the door swung wide, they stepped inside the dim entry, looking over their shoulders. The low-ceilinged room, the din of conversation, closed around them like shadows. "We'll figure this out. We'll find our way back home," Jorit said, hoping it was true. "Or at least we can find some food."

Inside the inn, they asked for the owner, hoping there would be work for them. When a woman came to help, two empty tankards in her arms, her hair cropped as short as Jorit's, Ania stared.

"Master Archivist! Sonoria?" Ania cried. "How?" She threw her arms around her mentor, while Jorit looked on guardedly. A tankard clattered to the floor.

The serving woman peeled Ania's arms from her shoulders. "What happened?" She stared at the clock they carried. "Why is that here with you? Is it damaged?"

Ania shook her head. "We were attacked in the library—the Pressmen—"

The Master Archivist winced as the inn's noise quieted. "Careful!" She looked at the women a long time. "You need a room."

"We have no money," Ania said.

"It's no charge. I want to hear what happened, and you look exhausted."

Jorit took the key Sonoria held out, but Ania stared. "That seems like a loss for the inn."

Sonoria, her face drawn and worried, shook her head. "Not nearly. I'll repay it. It's far too easy to live here, knowing what will affect market prices. The innkeeper is a widower and was happy to have me to help out." She handed them each several coins. "I'd hoped, one day, to find my way home. You can take these safely, buy some clothes. But with a warning. You mustn't try to change too much. You cannot stop the Pressmen here. Or any other time in the past."

"Why not?" Ania held on to the Archivist's hand, as if she didn't believe the woman was real.

"Because I tried, here, to break the press before it became too powerful. I pushed one of their leaders, and he fell against the machine." Sonoria's eyes glazed with the memory. "And once I'd caused his death, though it was an accident, time cannot forget an event that big. I can never move farther in the future than that last moment I was in the library before I am sent back. The past has already happened, and because I made it happen, I have to be here."

She wiped her eyes with her sleeve. "Listen to me, Ania. You can't change the past, no matter how much you want to. It's already happened. Trying to do so overmuch will trap you here." The Master Archivist spread her arms wide to encompass the inn. "Like me."

Ania stared, trying to comprehend. "Trapped?" A customer greeted the Master Archivist by an unfamiliar name. "You mean you can't come with us?"

Sonoria frowned. "I never traveled with the clock; I adjusted its settings to move back and forth in time for a certain period." She lifted a small pendant with a cracked, pale piece of opal set in a small bezel. "From the back of the gem. When my time was up, it would return me to the library. But when I made my mistake, trying to interfere with the Press's past instead of its future, the piece of gem I traveled with cracked. And then I found I was stuck."

All those times Sonoria had vanished. All the times she'd refused to meet with the deans. "You were trying to keep the Pressmen at bay?" Ania grasped Sonoria's hand, tears filling her eyes.

"I felt I had to. I'd finally discovered what was powering their campaign to unify knowledge. It's a gem, Ania. A fake gem that wants—needs—ink in order to continue to exist."

Ania was quiet while Sonoria's words sank in. A gem. Like the shopkeeper had said. "A real gem and a fake gem." The three books she carried in her satchel from the library felt even heavier now. "And you tried to destroy one with the other." Her face lit up. "I should have seen it before," she whispered.

If she'd learned nothing from antiquity, it was this: the

hardest changes to see are those happening all around you, until it's too late. "There must be a way to help." She had a second opportunity to rescue the library, and maybe Sonoria as well.

The Master Archivist watched her carefully, eyes searching Ania's. She pressed her lips together before she spoke. "I thought so too, once I realized what was happening and I discovered the clock's peculiarities. The gem can only travel where it's been before. Now the same is true for me. I've spent a lot of time wandering. But I failed to destroy the press. Failed to bind its gem. And trying to break it? Trapped me here."

"How might you be freed from this?" Jorit asked. She'd seen Ania's face.

"I don't know if I can be," Sonoria said. Ania didn't let go of Sonoria's hand, not until Sonoria pulled away. "When you return home, be sure to remember me somehow. Time doesn't forget events, but memory, especially for time travelers, is less precise."

"We don't know how to return home!" Jorit said. "Show us how the clock works."

Ania looked at her companion sharply. "Jorit!" But she wondered. Could they take Sonoria with them?

"It's all right," Sonoria said. "I've had plenty of time to consider my fate. It really is fine."

She reached for the clock. "You tell it to go by turning the harvest knob. At least that's how I did it. Set a span of time you want to be gone for." Her fingers pointed at the dials. Hovered. "According to an old book, you can try talking to it too, but that never worked for me."

Ania nodded, saying nothing about her heartbeats and the clock's pace.

Sonoria continued. "Do this for me: for all the books, for those of us who cultivate learning and debate, not just facts."

"What is it?" Ania said. "Anything. If it will help you."

"Find the Pressmen's gem and the printing press. In your present, not in the past. Destroy the press. Change the future before that disappears too."

Sonoria's fingers shook. She reached for the clock, then hesitated as if she was trying to hold back. "Remember when I told you that books started disappearing?" she said.

Ania nodded. "I was thinking about that. It happened in this era. There are references to texts, but not the texts themselves, mostly from Quadril, around the same time as the Pressmen began marching."

"I apprenticed at the library while trying to find one of those books—one my great-grandmother often cited in her diary—that never made it through to the modern era. A dictionary of gems."

"*The Book of Gems*?" The copy Ania had found was in her knapsack.

Sonoria nodded. "That was one of the first books I rescued. There are only two copies left, and no one else has seen it."

I've seen it, the clock whispered. *I'm in it.*

Ania jumped. But, thank the hordes, Jorit and Sonoria didn't notice her jitters. "Does nothing last?"

"Not even gems—look at how many are left from the Jeweled Valley. . . . One? Two?"

Two, came the whisper.

Ania shook her head as if a bug sang in her ear. "The shopkeeper said several. The Pressmen's record says none are left. The list of destroyed gems—contains almost all."

"But some survived," Sonoria said. She was gripping the clock now. And the clock's ticking had slowed to a crawl. "I wonder."

Be careful, we could be trapped if she breaks the mechanism. The whisper grew louder.

Ania tried to pull the timepiece away, her face pained. "You can't."

"I need to . . . ," Sonoria whispered, staring at the clock, "try. Once more."

Jorit and Sonoria both gripped the clock. Ania pulled at the Master Archivist's sleeve, then grabbed the clock's thick base and pulled. The three of them fought in the inn to gain a firm handhold on the clock.

There was a loud crack as it slipped from their fingers and crashed to the ground.

Oh no. Jorit dove to scoop up the splintered case. She pressed pieces of wood back to the box. The harvest knob broke off and rolled free.

The inn's customers stared at the scuffle.

Meanwhile, the fire opal glowed inside the cracked gearbox, the twisted gears.

"I might go home!" Sonoria Vos's fingers scrabbled for the gem behind the clock face.

But the opal became brighter, as if it caught the setting sun's light. The Master Archivist pulled her fingers back. Stuck them in her mouth, even as she teetered on her heels. *"Hot."*

The gem seemed to whisper, words, names. Sonoria reeled and toppled, disappearing even as her arms reached out for Ania. And then she was gone. Just like—Ania remembered now—the Pressman had disappeared from the library.

Ania bit her lip to keep from screaming, though she could not hear herself over the roaring in her ears. *Sonoria. Again. Lost.*

The inn was too quiet. The customers staring at them, mouths gaping, focused on her. On the broken timepiece. On the space where Sonoria—their friend—had been.

This time, Ania felt the loss in her fingertips and her heart. She felt something else too. She felt the pulse of the gem, the ache of it. As if the opal was hurting as well. The whisper came again. *I tried to help.*

Ania swallowed hard.

That voice. So familiar, from the library. Now here too. The opal whispered to her.

What was more likely? That an opal tried to send Sonoria back to the library? That it was talking to her? Or that she was going mad?

As Jorit gingerly lifted all the clock's pieces that she could hold, Ania said, "We can fix it." The inn's clients turned back to their food.

Jorit handed the clock to Ania as the inn resumed its normal hum and churn.

Ania cradled the opal in its nest of bent gears, saying again, "We can fix this. I know it." *We can find her, we can rescue the books. We can save the opal.* Her words ticked like a clock, struggling to stay regular.

Breathe. You cannot change time.

She closed her eyes and heard the opal's whispers, faint but there. The words shifted and ran strangely, as if the opal's thoughts—but how could an opal think?—were cracked also. "*Shhhh,*" Ania whispered, trying to loop calm thoughts around herself and the gem both at the same time.

She felt a tug on her thoughts, as if she was being pulled into the gem. The tug was familiar, like being pulled through time, a thread through a needle. Ania did not want to go, not yet. She struggled, fighting the pull. The gem whispered a single word: "*Lapidary.*" Then retreated into itself, and the pulling ceased.

Silence, for the first time since—Ania realized it had been since she had come to work at the library for the Master Archivist.

The gem. This whole time, it had been the gem whispering to her. Not some memory of Sonoria Vos.

Once more, Ania sucked in her breath at the loss of her friend. It felt like fire. As hot as the opal had. Jorit put a hand on Ania's shoulder. She didn't say anything, but the warmth of her fingertips through the fabric was comforting.

Lapidary. What did that mean? The shopkeeper had said she had the look of one. The opal—no, she'd imagined it. "Speak again," she whispered.

But the opal was cooling now, its colors fading to pale reflections. The gem was cracked—was it breaking? Not dying. It couldn't die, could it?

Like people couldn't disappear, lost in time. Books couldn't suddenly go blank.

Ania stifled a low groan. A whispered *no*.

They would be trapped here—and now—forever if the gem was broken.

~

The two women retreated to their room. The innkeeper had grumbled about not being able to keep staff when Sonoria's absence was noticed. Then he'd watched with curiosity as she and Jorit had tried to repair the broken clock.

"Can you fix it?" Ania looked at Jorit.

"With tools, and time." Tools they had. Jorit opened her lock-picking kit. There were tweezers and pliers in the felt roll. But did they have time?

"Sonoria—" Ania caught her breath. Seeing her had been a blow. Losing her again was almost unbearable, despite how she'd changed. "She said the gem could not go anywhere or when it hadn't been before."

"So the valley."

"And the library."

"And Quadril."

"Possibly others, but if we want to get somewhere new, we're going to have to travel the old-fashioned way. And perhaps the other gem—the emerald—made the same trip—at least the valley and Quadril and here. "

In order for them to make the same journey, Ania realized, she would need to accept the fact of the fire opal. The whispers. That she could hear them. She shivered, then pretended to look in her satchel, hiding her confusion from Jorit. She was a librarian. Not a lapidary.

And Jorit? What was Jorit? She'd been more than a thief, once. Ania lifted the shawl and counted the books she carried. *The Book of Gems. The Visitors' Guide to the Jeweled Valley. A Dictionary of Riverward.* She'd been carrying her past with her the whole time.

The innkeeper came to their room then, carrying bread and tea, looking frazzled. "I am a bit short staffed," he apologized.

Ania swallowed hard and handed him a coin from the handful Sonoria had given her. Jorit waited until he left to speak.

"We don't know much, then. The clock has moved to protect us, and itself, each time. Sonoria told us how we might guide it, but we don't know how to fix it." Jorit's voice was tinged with sadness. "What if we could go back to a specific time and place?"

"You lost your brother in the Eastern Shores?" Ania's voice was level, but she paid attention to how Jorit answered. She felt her own losses sharply. Tried to imagine how much Jorit's had cost her.

Jorit sighed. "If I could help him now? Make him well before we fled?" She busied her hands, making a last adjustment on the modified clock. Bending back a gear. Hoping the crack in the gem didn't mean terrible things. Then she wrapped her hands around the clay tea mug. "I understand your sadness. Losing someone twice."

Ania gripped Jorit's fingers and her tea mug. The warmth returned to her own hands. She closed her eyes and they both grieved for a moment.

The clock had saved them. But to what end?

Ania sniffled again. She reached inside her bag again and lifted the books out. "Copies."

"What?"

"We can make copies. Of the books. Like Sonoria did. She said there were only two copies of *The Book of Gems* left. If we scatter many of that book, and others, they will not be lost as quickly. We can keep them in circulation."

"Isn't that altering something here?"

Ania shook her head slowly. "Not if we don't change anything in the texts, I think. We're not altering. Just copying." She grinned. "Maybe it will work. Until the clock is fixed, anyway."

Jorit shook her head, trying to understand.

As they rested and regained their strength at the inn, the timepiece remained quiet, the gem, pale within its bent setting. Unable to move them any farther, no matter how many different combinations of "get us out of here" the pair tried.

They were stuck.

The inn—despite lacking modern conveniences—wait.

Ania stopped herself. For its time, it was very modern. Indoor plumbing, gas lanterns. Light to work by and no need to deal with bedpans. Only a long walk down a cold passage to the washroom in the evening, in the dark of the creaky inn. The inn was very comfortable for its period. At least for the three nights they'd been able to pay in advance.

It was more that she and Jorit were not comfortable in this time.

~

When Ania rose in the middle of the night, Jorit remained curled up on the far side of the cot, snoring. She briefly considered asking the thief to accompany her to the washroom, but decided that waking her was too much to ask, even if their friendship felt stronger now.

Ania slipped on her gown and put the clock in her pocket out of habit.

The clock ticked unevenly. The restless, cracked gem whispered. As it had all night, beneath her pillow. Ania's relief that the gem was all right was tinged with the need to sleep. Still, the whispers came: *Listen, lapidary.*

She stepped from her room and instantly regretted that decision. A floorboard creaked loudly, and she heard a door open.

"What have we here?" The innkeeper stepped suddenly from the staircase.

"What indeed but a patron wishing to relieve herself?" Ania said. Her voice was calm, but her heart raced. The innkeeper had seemed nice enough downstairs. Now, in the waiting darkness, she wondered if that had been a ruse.

Ania felt the timepiece begin to tick irregularly and decidedly faster as the man moved closer. He put a hand out to touch her arm.

The clock's ticking grew louder. *No, not here. Don't jump time here, without Jorit.*

Ania backed quickly into her room and locked the door, without waking her travel companion from sleep. She pulled the timepiece from her pocket—the ticks had slowed again. "We nearly left her here!"

That couldn't happen. She thought of the professors in the square, Sonoria.

She wouldn't abandon anyone again.

It won't happen again, whispered the clock. *I promise.*

"Who are you? What are you?"

When the clock didn't answer, Ania buried herself in her side of the bed, blankets over her head, and tried to drown out the clock's ticks.

She heard Jorit settle again, muttering something to herself, but then she was quiet.

Beneath Ania's pillow, the clock kept a more regular pace, though the gem had still looked pale when she peered behind the latch. It did not whisper again.

Finally, as sunlight edged the windowpane, Ania slept.

TESTIMONY OF FORMER PRESSMAN XACHAR OUBLIANT
BEFORE THE COMMISSION ON
KNOWLEDGE AND LOYALTY
INTERIM REPORT

Special attention should be paid by future histories of recent events to the following excerpts of one exchange between the commission and the student-turned-Pressman Xachar Oubliant:

Commissioner Varr: "Young man, you claim to have become overpowered by circumstance."

The former student shifts in his chair so much that the metal seat creaks. "It's the truth. I didn't intend—"

Commissioner Andol: Intentions are not actions. Intentions don't leave a mark on history. What was your role with the Pressmen? Did you collaborate with the librarian and the thief? What will you do now?

Xachar Oubliant plays with a small chip of pale green glass hung from a cord around his neck. He shrugs.

Commissioner Varr: "That is no answer."

He raises his green eyes to the three commissioners. Speaks so simply that the commission is compelled to believe he means it when he says, "Sirs, I will do what is useful. That's what I've always done."

Commissioners' Note: Among those we've questioned, young Oubliant is by far the most willing to cooperate with our work. This is admirable.

8.

Xachar

By his fifth day as the assistant Presskeeper, Xachar was in love.

If one can be said to love a machine.

Whispers followed him into the Pressmen's mess hall. He paid no mind. He'd made no friends in the barracks. He wouldn't need any. He had the press itself. No one else had that. Not even those who'd tended the machine before him, now manning the lesser presses. They'd been broken by the Midnight Emerald, Xachar knew. But he was stronger. His mind was clearer after a workday than it had been the day before.

He felt their gazes like the sun on the back of his neck. Watched when others spread their packs across chairs so he could not sit near them. He was marked. He knew that too. With his ink-lined fingernails, he could trace any jar or menu and the words would begin to disappear. By the end of his second week, they made him wear gloves to the mess hall. And everywhere else.

The ink dust that he pulled from the press's scuppers glowed a little, but only on the darkest nights. It was nearly impossible to wash it all off. Xachar, as he walked back to the pressroom from the mess hall that evening of no stars and no moon, gleamed like the gem at the heart of the press.

Instead of going to the barracks to sleep, he returned to the room, to the always-running press. The ink dust scuppers were full again. The gem was a dark, oily color.

"You've been busy," he murmured. He didn't expect the gem to reply, and it did not.

Down the hall, shouts erupted. Pressmen stood to see what the commotion was. Xachar stuck his head out of the room and watched as the First Leader, who had been in office for only eleven months, was clamped at the elbows and sides and carried unceremoniously from her office.

They marched past Xachar's door. "Careful," the leader hissed. "You'll be next."

More men streamed past. Xachar stopped one of them. "What did the leader do?"

"Former leader. Failure to unify knowledge, I believe." He sounded happy. "The second captain will address the corps." They walked out of Xachar's line of sight, the former First Leader still struggling.

When they returned, they collected Xachar too, in the same manner.

They lifted him high, fingers bunching the fabric of his Pressmen's blue uniform, bruising the skin beneath. They took him down a long set of stairs and into the basement, where they put him in a room alone and locked the door.

"Why do you do this?" Xachar asked over and over. "All I want—" He paused. This far from the press, his mind clouded with doubts. He began to feel an edge of fear. He'd been important, above, before the leadership change. What was he now?

By the ink-dusted, fading glow of his skin, Xachar watched a rat run across the opposite wall. It clutched a shred of blank paper in its teeth. A damp stain spread across the dark, uneven ceiling. He smelled something rank and heard a mad laugh echo down the basement hallway from another room. His ears caught a mechanical sound—but it was only the edge of a lock turning metal against metal.

And as the hours turned into one long night, Xachar's dust-layered glow began to fade. Darkness gathered around him.

Then footsteps. A lock's turn. Xachar shook himself awake.

The figure who knelt beside him was none other than the lead officer from the Far Reaches campaign. He recognized the man's voice from speeches at Gladulous Hall.

"You have fixed the Great Press before, have you not?"

Xachar nodded. He cleared his throat, trying to find his voice.

The officer didn't wait. "What is your loyalty to the First Leader? To the Pressmen? To Knowledge?"

Xachar looked up at him, confused. They were obviously no longer all the same thing. He thought for a moment. A lie could be the end of him. Choosing wrong also. "My loyalty is to the Great Press," he finally acknowledged, using the officer's name for it.

"That is a better answer than most." The man lifted Xachar up by his shirt. "You are still needed."

On the stairs, the officer made him swear to another First Leader—the third such in two years. "You'll be guarded night and day," the man added—but did not tell him anything more until they reached the pressroom hallway.

"I understand," Xachar said. Although he didn't. Not yet.

Along the wide hallway, the former Pressmen's chairs sat empty. The printing presses of Knowledge had ground to a halt. The officer saw Xachar glance twice at the empty chairs and shook his head.

The silence from the pressroom felt as thick as storm clouds. "What did you do?" Xachar whispered. How long had he been in the basement?

"Yesterday, while you were . . . occupied, the former First Leader tried to reassemble part of the press, to make it work faster. She . . . failed." The officer shrugged. "The Pressmen are now governed by a ruling committee of fifteen, who advise the first leader and will all make decisions regarding how the press is run. Our first decision was to have the original functions restored. It's only been a few days. You will be able to fix it quickly."

He opened the door, and Xachar stepped through. The room was dark. He knew the gem would be ice-pale before he checked. "Get me all the remaining books with print on them still in storage. Even those with Knowledge if you have to."

"But—"

"Do you want the press running? Do you want to be able to continue to distribute Knowledge?"

It was enough. The officer backed away, and soon a cart full of books arrived.

Xachar busied himself with sorting out what had happened. There was another bent gear, two more wheels added. And the ghost of a gem at the press's center, he reminded himself. He needed to prepare to see that. He removed the unnecessary parts from the press and laid them carefully nearby, in case he required them later.

The press was clogged with ink. No one had cleaned

out the scupper. A wad of paper had worked its way in between the gear shaft around where the emerald was hidden, like a cocoon. Xachar's teeth clenched in anger.

He found the Pressmen's tools where he'd left them—they'd been shoving books into the feeder without any tune-ups. Xachar muttered and shook his head. He pulled the paper away from the emerald's setting. And gaped.

The Midnight Emerald had grown quickly. Had the Pressmen had been overfeeding it, trying to make it work faster? During the time that Xachar had spent in the basement, it had nearly doubled in size. Its facets had the oil sheen of a polished gem, but parts of it looked new and raw. It was ghost-pale, starved of ink, but it had grown. Up and around the press frame.

The cart arrived, the officer pushing it himself. "We've scoured the barracks and the town. Unless there are books secreted away, no one in Quadril has any more."

Will this be enough for now? Xachar wondered.

The officer seemed to read his mind. "It has to be enough. If we stop distributing Knowledge, there will be insurrection, and then who knows what will happen to the Great Press."

From within the pressworks, Xachar heard something, or thought he did. A voicelike rustling. He'd heard it in his dreams too. His jaw tightened at the thought of the press being destroyed. What would the Midnight Emerald suffer, without ink? A vision came: the hallway, emptied of blank-eyed Pressmen. What would become of Quadril?

He had to protect it all—Quadril and the Midnight Emerald, both.

The whispering continued. "Yes," Xachar heard himself saying. "Yes, I think I can help you find the hidden books. Let me get a pen."

The gem, it turned out, remembered every ounce of ink it had sucked from the now-blank books, the shapes letters took when they were laid on the page, and the words' sounds. It remembered the smell of other books besides those it had wiped clean. And where those books had been. The books those books had been shelved next to. All it had to do was whisper to Xachar, and the remaining books—thousands of them, hundreds of thousands—could be revealed from their hiding places.

Xachar stayed in the press room for a full week writing the list by hand. When he gave it to the new leader, it was a hundred pages long.

"We'll find them for the mighty press," the Pressmen's leader said.

Xachar smiled. The emerald would be pleased to have more ink as it grew.

9.

Jorit

While Ania slept, her pillow muffling the damaged time-piece, Jorit made mental lists of Where, When, and What.

Four locations: the library, the valley, the Pressmen's parade, the market. Four eras: their present, hers and Ania's; their ancestors' lost past; and two with possible connections to the fire opal and its surviving mate, the Midnight Emerald. If Sonoria's story was true.

No time to guess at that. Assume it true.

Jorit tiptoed to the other side of the cot and slipped the clock from beneath Ania's pillowed head. "Where else have you been, you lovely creature?"

A normal gem could not answer. And Jorit knew she couldn't possibly hear one of the mythical gems.

She laughed at herself for trying.

But Ania turned over in her sleep and began to murmur again.

Soon, Jorit could hear distinct words. She bent close and listened as sunrise turned the room's edges golden.

"A thousand places, a thousand years. Not much time." It was Ania speaking, but not Ania's cadence, not her accent. It sounded like the accent Jorit had heard from the other day. Jorit jumped and nearly dropped the clock again.

"You asked, I will answer," the voice continued, through Ania. "The watchmaker who made me is a good man. But gems change a person. He's a tinkerer. And I am many gems, and more than that. I survived." There was a long pause. "I haven't spoken in so long. Exhausting."

And then nothing.

"Please speak again," Jorit said.

No more words came from Ania's lips. The clock ticked unevenly.

Jorit nestled the clock beneath the pillow again so Ania would not know. The puzzle was getting more strange, not less. And now she couldn't sleep either.

On the only shelf in the room, three books were piled one on top of the other. When she lifted them up, they came away with a small tug, their cloth covers sticky with dust. The shelf beneath the books was two shades darker than the rest of the wood. The book pile hadn't been moved for some time.

She opened the top book, listening to the spine crackle. *A Dictionary of the Riverward.* Handwritten.

The next book was mostly blank; a few pages had very faded, illegible text.

The third, like the others, and like the banners and signs around the marketplace and the banners in the Eastern Shores, had been handwritten. *The Visitors' Guide to the Jeweled Valley*, it read.

Jorit looked closer. She'd seen it before in the library, but now she realized that the byline was a familiar Far Reaches surname—S. Vos. The handwriting had a modern tilt, closer to her own and Ania's.

She thought for a moment and smiled sadly. *Copies.*

She left Ania sleeping and went downstairs, to where the inn and tearoom had boasted a small library. The books there were well dusted; the spines were illegible.

"Those are books that survived the silvering," the innkeeper said, proudly coming up behind her. "We saved them by putting them in a lead case."

"What's the silvering?"

"A while back, someone noticed words disappearing from paper—a new kind of moth or something. There was no stopping it. Some of our books were completely ruined."

"Moths caused this?" Jorit held up the book from

her room to show she understood completely. "It's been happening in the Far Re—where I'm from too." She realized that if she said Far Reaches and someone were to check, there would be no evidence of it. Not yet.

But the innkeeper nodded. "It's the only logical explanation. There have been reports from nearby lately, and I know you came in town on foot. It's not rare anymore." He shrugged. "Not a lot of people read around here, so it's not too noticed. But I read, sometimes to the guests. They like to come to the hall, or trade gossip and then listen to the stories."

"What about books in the upstairs rooms?" Jorit asked. "Did any survive?"

A creak on the upstairs hallway, and the early morning quiet was broken. "No books in the rooms. They'd be used for"—he frowned—"waste paper."

"These must have wandered, then," Jorit said, handing *The Visitors' Guide* and the dictionary to the innkeeper. She kept the blank book. Ania had wanted to make copies.

The man grumbled about needing more help keeping order, but put the books into the case and then headed into the kitchen.

Ania descended the stairs, the light catching her clothes and the clock she carried in her hands.

"I had the strangest dreams," Ania whispered, glaring at the innkeeper's back.

Jorit looked at her, the truth waiting behind her teeth.

Ania continued. "But I haven't slept so well in a long time."

"You talked in your sleep, Ania," Jorit finally said. "You don't remember anything?" She wasn't sure if she wanted Ania to remember or not.

Ania shrugged, as if talking in her sleep was a silly thing. "Only dreams. Of the valley, long ago." But her brow wrinkled for a moment. Jorit wondered if she was holding things back.

Now's no time for keeping secrets, Jorit thought. But Ania didn't want to discuss it, so she wouldn't press. Jorit stayed silent.

The innkeeper returned and absently handed them each a stiff piece of toast—still stale tasting even with the crisp heat and a thick layer of butter applied—and took another coin from Ania. "Our serving woman was curious about the books too, a while back. Don't come from nearby, do any of you?" He made a small, almost disapproving sound with his tongue against her teeth.

Ania shook her head. "A long way away." She sounded fierce.

"You'll want to be getting on soon, then," the innkeeper whispered. "There've been a lot of fights here. Disappearances. No place for women traveling alone."

Jorit's face turned red. "That's rather archaic—"

But Ania stepped on her foot. "All right," she said. "We'll take our payment back, then."

The innkeeper gladly gave it, and they went to pack their bags.

When they were out on the street, Jorit fumed. "The nerve, the assumption."

"The times." Ania shook her head. "And that innkeeper. I'm old enough—" She stopped. "Unless—look." A handwritten poster on the wall described local thieves . . . two women, last seen traveling together. A reward for the return of a missing timepiece. Also described.

"The shopkeeper," she said. The innkeeper had done them a kindness, not turning them in. But others might have. "We have to get out of here. Before we can't any longer."

It isn't safe, she thought.

"But the books here survived the first erasures—there are clues here," Jorit said.

The clock in Ania's hand seemed to tick louder as they argued. But the ticking was unsettled. Off kilter.

Finally, Jorit put her hand on Ania's shoulder. She wouldn't let anything happen to the librarian, not until she understood more. "We need to leave in our own time. Deep breath." She began walking, pulling Ania along.

Ania took a deep breath. Then another. Finally, the clock's ticking slowed.

It's not me the clock is keeping safe, Jorit realized. *It's Ania.*

10.

Xachar

With a new supply of ink and books, the gem continued to grow. The new Pressmen regime reveled in this. "It is a sign of our better leadership," they announced to the barracks. They didn't mention Xachar.

Occasionally, a team would return from abroad and bring pieces of the emerald back with them. They'd pass the ink-laden gem sections through the door and Xachar would lay these atop the rest of the gem overnight.

The next morning, the pieces of gem would be incorporated into the whole, and the entire gem would darken by several shades.

Each time this happened, on the room's far side, the Midnight Emerald overtook more of the press. A facet gouged a whole in the wall. Xachar dreamed once that the gem grew over him while he slept.

That's when Xachar stopped taking naps near the press. He stopped sleeping well in the dorms either as the press began to creak under the weight.

If you keep it running, it won't hurt you.

Xachar couldn't think of his family. He thought hard about the mess he was in to avoid remembering his aunt's face, her mind wiped clean like a blank page, imagining the others lost somewhere in the bowels of the Pressmen's camp. He tried to look for them, had asked once and been laughed at. Everyone thought he was strange. No one of consequence.

Worse, he had a much more immediate problem than the fear he felt for his family.

The bigger the Midnight Emerald got, the more ink it required. And as far as Xachar could tell, there wasn't much ink remaining aside from the *Universal Compendiums of Knowledge* themselves.

Xachar attempted once to explain to the press that ink was a finite resource. He felt ridiculous talking to a gem. He tried mixing more ink himself, requisitioning new ink from elsewhere. But nothing worked the same way as ink that had already formed a word on a page. The press rejected it.

The day a book on the history of gems made its way to the pressroom, Xachar had tried to read up, to discover how to logic with the gem. He only got to the part where they whispered, where they controlled minds, before the second captain caught him at it.

"You don't need that," she said. "We have the manual and the *Universal Compendiums of Knowledge.*" As Xachar watched, she fed the book to the press herself. Her long fingers grazed the press's intake wheel, and she yelped. Pulled her hands away just in time.

Xachar hadn't believed a word he read of the now-lost book. Still, to spite the second captain, he tried to remember what the chapter he'd been reading had said. He decided that if they could whisper and control minds, gems could also listen.

So he started speaking to the Midnight Emerald again. On long, cold evenings in Quadril when the rest of the squad was in the barracks, Xachar told the Midnight Emerald all the news from abroad.

He began reading to the press, and the gem, from books before he fed them in.

He spoke so much, his voice grew hoarse, which was fine because he didn't have anyone else to talk to. In the dormitories, other Pressmen avoided him. Said he was too sallow, too odd. Not a real Pressman, even though he did the hardest of jobs.

And to his great delight, the gem stopped growing, stopped working its way over the press's struts, stopped growing like a hornets' nest underneath.

But the gem's low ebb-and-flow thrum never stopped. When Xachar was out of the room, he longed for the sound. He took a spare cot down to the pressroom so he could tend the machine and its gem night and day. The gray canvas and wood sling fit against the far wall, out of the gem's reach.

Dangerous, sure, but Xachar didn't want anyone else tending the press.

Soon, he slept there all the time. He was no longer nervous.

When the captain learned of Xachar's new habits, he entered the pressroom without knocking. "Are you certain? Even after what happened to the others?" He caught Xachar bent over the press, fixing an intake cylinder.

Without rising, Xachar nodded. "No one's spent as much time with the press as I have. And I'm not ill." On the contrary, both he and the press were doing better than ever.

His clothes were sweat stained, and his skin had taken on the sheen of an ink drum, but operations were moving faster than ever.

So fast that they were once again running out of books for the press, and out of the ink that the press needed. The captain noticed. And Xachar noticed him noticing.

But the gem had yet to pale.

"We'll double *Compendium* production tonight," the captain said. "The gem can take it. The new Pressmen territories need copies."

Xachar straightened, wiped his hands on his pants, and frowned. "That will require more books in the end." Were there more books somewhere?

"We'll do another pass through the territories," his captain said. "There are surely still some that people have been hiding." The Pressman glared at the emerald. "Greedy thing."

The press and the emerald that bore it seemed to list toward the door. Xachar found himself with his hand on the knob, his back against the heavy oak, blocking the Pressman's exit.

"No," he whispered. The room turned dark green. Ink shadows curtained his eyes.

Xachar woke in the room with the press. His hands bloodstained. Gore in his hair. The sound of pounding on the door outside.

"Locked! The madman's locked it. He's in there with the press."

"Where's the Pressman?"

"Xachar, where's the captain?"

A whispered "You won't believe it when you see him—like the color's drained right out of the man. Spooky." Then, louder: "We should break open the door!"

Xachar looked at his hands again. They were pale, but stains dark as ink ran beneath his nails.

And the press—the Midnight Emerald nearly covered half of it, and was much darker. What had happened? Had he finally gone as mad as the others? Xachar felt fine.

Keep it running.

No. Xachar felt better than fine. He could sense things now—ink and paper. He could hear the rustling of treasured books hidden throughout Quadril.

The Midnight Emerald whispered too, and Xachar could hear its hunger.

He wanted books and ink for the press. For the campaign. For the Midnight Emerald. But they were outside. And between him and outside were several Pressmen.

How to get out and find what he needed, without being caught.

Many days ago, in the main square of Far Reaches University, Pressmen had blown ink dust in the faces of those who disagreed with them.

Xachar remembered the blank looks on professors' faces. He checked the bin where printing dust and lint collected. Nearly empty. That wouldn't help.

But. The press itself. The books were stripped blank when they ran through the machine.

Could the press work on other kinds of knowledge? Xachar wondered silently, and the answer came loud and clear. *Yes. All kinds.*

The press smelled of grit and grime, blood, ink, and

memory, all tied together, all enough to bring a thing alive.

Xachar slowly unlocked the door. He looked out at the Pressmen on the other side.

"I need to show you something," he said. "Please come in."

And he and the press waited for the others to enter.

11.

Ania

The clock's ticks sounded strange to Ania. Weaker. *Tick-tick*, pause. *Tick-tick*, pause. The first tick slow and sibilant, as if the mechanisms were struggling. The second, fast and short. Then she heard the whisper. *Si-ma*. A cadence much like the ticking.

Sima. Sima Sima Sima. A rhythm, not a whisper.

She put her hands to her ears, but the sound continued. Jorit looked at her, worried. Tugged on her sleeve. "We have to go."

Sima. Was it a word? She'd asked the clock a question back at the inn—was it answering? What did that word mean?

Ania blinked. She'd seen the word somewhere. In *The Book of Gems*, the catalog of names of all the jewels and their lapidaries?

As Jorit led her away from the market and the inn, and down a shadowed lane, Ania pulled the catalog from her satchel and looked. Yes, the youngest lapidary. The last one to have her name recorded by the Valley Jewels: Sima.

Ania couldn't find any more information—other lapidaries were connected with a major gem, their skill with it documented. Ania paged through the book as she and Jorit walked toward the town walls. The whispers matched the crunch of their footfalls on the paving stones. *Sima.*

Ania replaced the book in her satchel and covered it again with the scarf. Jorit kept tugging her forward, the clock beneath her arm, fingers firmly wound around Ania's dark sleeve.

As they sped away from the town, Ania thought about her heritage, about the stories of her grandmother: so many times the family had fled before the Pressmen and, before that, other armies. She'd witnessed the beginning of one such wave, with the Pressmen's parade. And she couldn't change the course of those marching feet. She could only try to run before them.

And Ania knew she was tired of running.

How her ancestors had been the last family to leave the Jeweled Valley. How they'd always been careful of who they'd taken into their confidences, preferring books to people. She'd once heard her grandmother whispering and listening to nothing and no one. How she'd hidden a handful of broken gems in her pocket and the family had locked her away in a spare room.

You have the look of a lapidary, the shopkeeper had said. She'd ignored him.

Now Ania stopped, pulling Jorit to a standstill. *Was* she a lapidary? Or what passed for one now that all the real gems were gone or broken? She could hear a voice. She'd talked to herself and ignored the answers that sometimes came since she'd begun working at the university library.

But now she knew. "This is one of the last gems," she said to Jorit.

"It's a strange one," Jorit said. "A powerful mix of stones. Could you find it in the book?"

Ania shook her head. "But I can hear it whispering," she finally admitted. "It has a name, and it can move across time. It could at least. Maybe never again." Her head ached with ticking.

"Ania! Don't slow down, not yet." Jorit pulled her and the clock farther from the town. Ania's braid fell around her shoulders. Their feet scuffed the rough pavers that were slowly transitioning into gravel and stone. Ania's toes caught a gap in the road. She faltered.

She could go no farther.

A stand of trees huddled at a bend in the road just ahead. Ania leaned that way. "I need to sit."

Jorit let her veer off the road, and soon Ania crouched in the shadows. She stared at the opal within the broken clock's sides.

She looked at Jorit. "I think this gem is more than air moving through crystal structures. I think . . ." She was trying to recall the Jeweled Valley's myths, among the books she'd memorized while trapped in the library. "I'm afraid."

"It's all right," Jorit said. "I'll keep you safe."

Ania strained to remember, but couldn't quite—something about the defeated kingdom, the sacrifice a lapidary had supposedly made for her Jewel.

Sima.

Jorit pulled the travel guide from Ania's pack. "'The Jewel and Her Lapidary'—I remember that formation from childhood," she said. "There was a lapidary named Sima. She was the last of them."

"Okay," Ania said, sweeping her long braid back over her shoulder. She lifted the broken gears from the stone and looked over the places where the gem had been altered to smooth the mechanisms, the escarpment. Her fingertip brushed the divot where a small piece of the opal had been cut away. Then she examined the break from the drop in the marketplace. "You've been through so much."

"What are you doing?" Jorit said, concerned. "Who are you talking to?"

Ania ignored her. She put her hand on the fire opal, whispering, "Sima. Is that your name?" Instead of the gem calling her, Ania called the gem. She held it in her mind and for a moment felt the pull through the needle's eye, but then she became the needle and the thread. She felt the gem encompass her mind, and she bound it, tightening the space between the crack, sealing it. "Sima."

When Ania opened her eyes, Jorit gasped. "Your eyes. They were brown, I'm sure. Now they're the color of opals. All colors."

For a moment, Ania saw her fellow traveler's face in facets, as a child and a young woman, as an old woman too. Jorit was beautiful.

Ania reeled. The trees spun around her dizzyingly, as saplings, as a bare meadow, as an ancient grove. "What is happening?"

A heartbeat later, she answered herself. "Time. I can see it."

A moment after that, she shuddered. "The gem can see it. Not me. I can see through the gem. And it's more than a gem. She—had a name—Sima." She paused, hoping Jorit would understand. "I was right. She was once a lapidary too—partly. The opal is a compendium." She caught her breath for a moment. "It's alive."

. She looked at the books they'd carried from the library, *The Book of Gems*, the travel guide. The books shifted beneath the opal's lens: they were so many things at once, a tree, a river, the blood of a child, the pages blank then inscribed with words, the gems inside all coming down to a secret Ania could not see, but the pages, the pages blurred and aged. . . .

She shook her head to clear it. Felt Jorit's arms around her shoulders, supporting her. The once thief, now friend, future—

Ania caught her breath.

Her friend now. Keeping her from toppling over in the dirt.

"What is it?" Jorit asked.

"I can see what the gem sees. I can understand, and it's difficult." Ania clutched her head as it began to ache. "But I understand better what happened to some of the books. They're being erased, the ink pulled right from them. I saw it at the university, but didn't understand. The Pressmen are using their gem to feed off the ink, the knowledge inside. The gem was trying to show us how the Pressmen are doing what they're doing, but it couldn't control when it was going any more than we could."

She clung to Jorit and saw what Sima saw. All the places the fire opal had been. All the moments in times past and future. For a moment, she was both Ania and Sima. She knew, in that moment, that they'd seen Sima's friend the Jewel Lin running from the palace. She knew all that had happened.

"It will be all right," Sima whispered, from Ania's lips.

"No! We must go back!" Ania countered, her eyes shut tight. The vein at her temple throbbed as she fought for the fire opal's attention. "To rescue Lin, to rescue Sonoria. To save the Pressmen."

"You cannot fight time," Sima said.

"We must go forward." Jorit tried to speak to the fire opal, to beg for help. But Ania needed to realize it too. "We cannot change the past. You saw what happened to the old Master. Do you want to be trapped in time like that?"

Ania's eyes opened, blazing. "That's my friend," she said. "I cannot leave her to die then."

"Sonoria? You can't remove her from then, not now," Jorit said. "She's trapped there, the clock—Sima—can't change that. Especially not after what happened. Sima fought back with everything she had. If you stay, you'll be trapped too, and the books, and possibly many other things, will disappear forever." Jorit waited. Then, when Ania didn't respond: "We have to go. Forward."

Ania's eyes filled with tears, but she nodded. "I know."

She and Jorit both grasped the broken clockwork. Ania heard the fire opal's wild, half-constrained whispers; they both felt its heart beating against their hands. Slowly an image formed in Ania's mind, of a far-flung future, with machines and masked guards. Of the library under siege, falling into its own basement.

"No," she whispered. "Sima, that's too far!"

It was too late. The clock ticks slowed and lengthened and, maddeningly, they echoed twice in Ania's ears, once for the opal, once for her. She shook, and Jorit's hand covered hers, steadying her. Then her free arm reached for Jorit's shoulder, and Jorit's free arm held her friend and the fire opal tight.

Pale clouds swirled around them, holes tearing in the mist. The broken clock and the opal within it returned them to the library's quiet.

In the empty clockroom's shadows, the sharp ticking of the big clock's sweep hand echoed like a knife hitting a glass. The small clock's broken, irreverent ticking bounced off the rhythm, and the close space filled with discordance.

Ania whispered, "The clock still works."

The fire opal had taken them to a different time than it had meant to. Earlier—before the Pressmen came into the university. The timepiece's repaired mechanisms weren't perfect yet.

Ania collapsed in her friend's arms, and Jorit wrapped her shawl around her until she stopped shivering. Finally, Ania opened her eyes.

"Brown again," Jorit whispered. She tucked strands of Ania's hair back into her braid.

The library's halls and stacks were dark except for the clock face's glow.

Ania looked at the glass. Unbroken. Numbers still there. The Master Archivist's name—and her grandmother's—clearly lettered on the clock face. *Ania Dem.*

The breath Ania drew shuddered so loudly that Jorit turned, worried.

"I'll be fine," she said.

"You're lying," Jorit answered, almost tenderly. "We have no time for lies. Not anymore."

Ania met Jorit's eyes. "We'll find the truth together." She calmed, and they moved toward the clock's mechanism.

The room was not yet filled with books. The Pressmen's demands had not yet begun. Ania's cot was there, but empty. She'd moved it that day, she remembered. The day the Master Archivist disappeared. Her name had been—

"Ania," Jorit whispered. "Focus."

They were still in the past, but not far in the past. Long enough back to travel to where the press was, and to arrive . . . in the present? The thought was confusing. Perhaps it would work.

"We have to get to Quadril. Fast. To stop the other gem," she said with more conviction than she felt.

Jorit nodded again, but this time with grave concern. "How?"

"I don't know. We don't have money for boat passage." Prices had been sky-high for a boat from the Far Reaches long before the danger was readily apparent. And there was no way to walk to Quadril from here.

Jorit frowned. Pulled out a handful of ancient coins. Her eyebrows shot up, and she looked at Ania. "I've given up thieving."

"Don't worry." Ania clasped her hand reassuringly. "Those were fairly gotten. We'll need money to repair the timepiece too."

"If we dare try to travel that way again." Jorit's eyes closed again. This time from exhaustion. She lay down on the cot beside Ania before she fell down.

As her eyes closed, the timepiece ticked faster.

"No," Ania whispered. She felt the pull of time, the thread drawing out. She fought it, but she was tired. Very tired.

"Wait—" Jorit cried out, reaching for the clock too, but late. And so slow.

The fire opal, the clock, and Ania all disappeared, leaving the cot with a dent and a slowly collapsing blanket.

~

When Ania woke, she was still in the library, but there were few books, and the clock . . . was a series of cogs laid out on the floor.

Ania gasped and hid in the stacks as Sonoria Vos strode past, dragging her young assistant with her.

The younger librarian's braid swung half loose, hairpins scattered behind her.

"Do you hear something?" the librarian asked.

"It's a library," the Master Archivist answered. "There are always whispers."

Ania knew she must not be seen. Too risky. She might accidentally change something big and be trapped forever, like her predecessor. And with the timepiece too.

She looked again at the floor. The small clock and its case sat there, new and shiny.

But she couldn't steal the parts without breaking the other clock.

She could copy them, though. Copies overcame time.

But only with books. And with clocks. Not people.

That she could travel back in time, but only to learn how to change the present, was a sharp, cold fact.

That night, Ania began to fix the broken clock, using scraps of metal, pieces of wood from elsewhere in the library. Her previous work among books about clockworks, many days spent traveling with a thief, and learning to live on her wits guided her and served her well.

During the day, she slept in the stacks, her robes turned out, like a student. Sometimes, she copied from memory one of the books she'd read while trapped in the future library. She hid these in the stacks. Sent some to other universities.

And when she was ready, she whispered to the gem, "Sima, wake up. Take us back to Jorit." She closed her eyes and thought of her friend alone in that library closer to the future than she was.

TESTIMONY OF LIBRARIAN ANIA DEM
BEFORE THE COMMISSION ON
KNOWLEDGE AND LOYALTY
INTERIM REPORT

Repeatedly, the librarian parries the commission's questions with her own. The tradition of academic discourse has its place, but in this, perhaps the Pressmen had it right. One story must emerge in order for there to be unity.

Commissioner Andol: Librarian Dem, your questions regarding the commission's authority in matters of history have distracted from your own baseless assertions about destroying a machine that endangered the Six Kingdoms, and your claims to have traveled in time. Without proof.

Librarian Dem: What would you undo if you could, Commissioner?

The librarian removes her dark glasses. Interrogates the commissioners with her eyes.

Librarian Dem: What will the record show once this business is done? And how will time remember you?

As a side note, for posterity, Commissioner Andol later mentioned that, despite speaking with her many times as her dean, he never noticed the peculiarity of Librarian Dem's eyes before. They are the colors of opals.

Librarian Dem: The past might be hidden or erased. Those who do the most to set things straight may not always be recalled. But they will have happened. They will have mattered. Time does not forget.

(Another side note: I confess again that I sputter at her audacity.)

Commissioner Andol: The record this commission crafts of events will be the standard for historians for the ages. It is important we get it right. Where are your loyalties?

Librarian Dem (taking another sip of water): Commissioner Andol, they are where they've always been. In the library.

Commissioner's addendum: There remain too many open questions regarding the librarian's testimony and her involvement in recent events. Until she and her companions can be compelled to provide more details of their activities for posterity, we will not include them in the official record.

12.

Jorit

Jorit, sitting on the floor beside Ania's empty cot, shook like a windblown page.

A clock ticked fast, then slow.

Between one moment and the next, the cot's frame creaked as Ania settled once again onto her side of the mattress.

"So tired." The voice was Ania's, but the accent was that of a long-ago lapidary.

Jorit, sitting beside her friend, smiled and smoothed the librarian's blanket, then her hair. "Sleep, then."

Ania closed her eyes, and soon her breathing slowed.

Meantime, Jorit's mind raced. She'd seen the clock break. She'd seen the Master Archivist disappear. She'd seen her friend's eyes change—now, sometimes, they were the color of the fire opal.

She'd seen Ania disappear, leaving Jorit more alone

than she'd felt since Marton had been carried away.

And the clock now? She lifted it in her hands. Almost as good as new. The fire opal was still cracked, but the rest of the gears and bindings worked.

Jorit chewed her cheek.

A woman with the eyes of a gem would be of great interest to the Pressmen. The gem's time manipulation and insight, even more so. The old Jorit might have said that was worth the price of safety. The Jorit who had lived through the past didn't agree.

She sat up straighter, to better guard the clock while her friend slept.

She knew more things now.

She'd heard the gem speak. She'd heard Ania argue with it.

Ania knew she could fight using time. Jorit was starting to understand this. And if time, then perhaps knowledge too.

She'd heard something joyous and desperate behind the gem's words when it fought with Ania. Gems could control things, but they liked being argued with . . . at least this one did.

"Sima," Jorit whispered. Silence was the only reply.

The former thief slumped to the floor. It had been worth a try.

The cot creaked again.

"Time," Ania whispered, and it was her voice, her accent now. She roused herself from the cot.

"To what?" Jorit replied.

"To leave," Ania said. She gathered books from the pile and several more from the stacks, then split these between her pack and Jorit's.

~

That night, the two women walked through Far Reaches University's gates, past the sleeping guards, and through town. The shell-pocked cobblestones crunched beneath their feet. The wind smelled of salt and waves.

As they headed toward the water, seagrass lined the road, scrub bushes dark against the deep blues of evening. A steamer's chimney billowed white smoke across the hued seascape. A bird clacked its beak. Jorit caught herself slowing down, enjoying the scenery, the moment.

"My brother used to say that the shared memories bound in the libraries of the Six Kingdoms could be used for a greater good, beyond university walls. He would have liked the original Pressmen, I think." She blinked in the sharp salt air.

Ania tugged at her hand. "We can't slow now, Jorit. If

we sail in the morning, we'll arrive a few weeks after we disappeared. I hope that's enough to avoid changing the past. Then we can catch the printing press and the gem inside."

Jorit shook her head. "You have a better sense of this than I do now." But she left her hand in Ania's for a moment. Then squeezed and let go as they approached the harbor.

At the main dock, several long wooden boats rode high in the water, their goods unloaded and carted away. Jorit tasted pepper in the air, smelled a husk of spices. She followed her nose to the ship that had come from a trading hub. "That one's from Quadril."

The captain of the *Farlook* took their money and gave them two canvas hammocks in the hold. The hammocks swayed with the tide and the wind, and Jorit and Ania slept for much of the journey. When they woke, they copied out versions of the books that Ania had memorized to the sound of sails flapping in the wind.

More than once, the rocking of the boat threw them together. They would lean on each other, steadying themselves. But not for too long.

Slowly the boat made its way down the coast. Slowly they sailed past Pressmen on the march on the shoreline. They tucked some of their books in with packages going ashore, kept others with them.

By the time they reached Quadril, they'd copied and scattered more volumes of *The Travelers' Guide* throughout the land, and while Jorit slept, Ania even managed to send two copies back in time with the gem's help.

As they approached the outskirts of Quadril, they saw smoke rising above blue and white flags near the docks. The Pressmen's barracks. Tents fanned out from several buildings at the center. Carts darted in and out, bearing books and people.

"I'd stay clear of that," the *Farlook*'s captain said. She waved another load of spices aboard as she spoke to Ania and Jorit. "Strange happenings. Heard some people have disappeared near there."

Jorit nodded. "We'll stay well clear." And they disembarked as the sun set behind the town.

Once it was dark, Ania and Jorit bribed their way onto a cart that was headed for the barracks. When they neared an area cordoned off with sawhorses and crate barricades, they saw a low building emitting glowing green smoke. The pair crouched down and slid out of the cart.

"That's it," the lapidary said. She started walking with Jorit toward the building.

Wait! Jorit bit back the word. She flexed her hand

against the clock instead. She patted Ania's arm, pulled on her hand. Her friend had started charging ahead since the fire opal began seeing with her eyes. "How will we get inside?"

"We have to figure out what it wants."

It . . . not them. *The gem. The emerald.* Jorit pulled Ania behind a tent. "We know what it wants. It wants books. Knowledge that doesn't belong to it." Her hand was gentle on Ania's wrist, but she wanted to pull the librarian far away, to safety. "It wants one unified voice that it can control."

Crouching low, Ania drew out the last three books they had. She looked at them intently, then at Jorit. Her eyes filled with concern. "I don't want these to be lost."

"Perhaps we can find more," Jorit said. But her face told a different story. There likely weren't any other books, not in all of Quadril.

"It had to be those books, my favorites, my treasures," Ania whispered. "Of course it did." She smiled sadly. She handed *The Book of Gems* to Jorit. Looked at her friend and touched her cheek. "I don't want anything to be lost."

Jorit shivered, then ran her fingers across the glittering cover. Opened the book, placed her palm against the old paper, the ink. "We'll find a way," she said, feeling the loss already. This was history; they'd discovered it, and now? Even she didn't want to give them up now.

Ania rose and walked straight up to the building with the odd glow, her shoulders set. She knocked on the door, looking around. A few guards stared at her from the shadows. They did not try to stop her.

"They're afraid," she muttered. "They have reason to be."

After a very long pause, one in which Jorit began looking for something to break the door, a lock turned. Hinges creaked. A sallow-faced young man answered.

Then Jorit knew they had no other option. The last books had to be bait. "You," she whispered. "From the library." *You betrayed us.*

The young man sucked his teeth. "You can't come in here." But his voice was soft, as if he very much did want Ania and Jorit to enter the pressroom.

"We can come in, Xachar," Ania said. Her eyes shone. "And we very much must."

The young man braced against the door. Ania pushed harder and Jorit pulled out *The Book of Gems*. She held it where the young man could see it. "I heard you were looking—"

The young man nearly salivated over the book. His fingers grazed the cover. "Where did you find this? We've been desperate. Gone to desperate measures."

When Ania pulled the book from his reach, Xachar lunged for it.

"You don't understand. This could save a life. Many lives if there are more."

"There are more, Xachar." Ania lifted the blank books into the light.

This time, Xachar grabbed Ania's arm and Jorit's robe, not the books. In a very different, stronger voice, he said, "I will show you why. I'll show you wonders."

Xachar pulled them down a hallway strewn with empty chairs and open doors to empty rooms. Ania thought the building had been abandoned until Xachar slowed near two figures wearing Pressmen blue, slumped on wooden chairs by a final closed door. Ania saw their hands and ankles had been tied to the wooden frames.

From beyond the door came a repetitive thunking. Despite the noise, Ania bit her lip to keep from making any sound.

Xachar didn't notice. He pushed the door open, then pulled the books from Ania's hands. Although the room was warm, the Pressman shivered. Without looking at the books' contents, Xachar fed *The Visitors' Guide* to the press first, pushing it beneath the rollers and sighing audibly as the second-to-last gem of the

Six Kingdoms hungrily drained the ink from the pages.

Ania stifled a groan. Jorit gritted her teeth. The thing was monstrous.

"That," whispered the fire opal with Ania's voice, into Jorit's ear, "is what you must destroy."

The press was overwhelmed by the emerald. No longer binding it, the gears were solely a source of ink production for the gem.

Jorit smelled the machine's inner workings as they heated up to devour another book—*The Book of Gems*. She blinked, recognizing the acrid scent of mining mixed with the richer tones of inks.

She could feel the gem's pulse—and hear its fragility. She looked more closely at it when Xachar wasn't paying attention.

Her miner's experience paid off—the emerald wasn't an emerald. It *was* colored glass. Leaded and fired, with shards of gemstones running through it. All the facets were stained dark—knowledge, ink, and blood curled through them like smoke.

"A fake," she muttered.

When the inked air around the gem drove her back, Jorit gagged. The smell, the taste of it in her teeth. She coughed then, and Xachar straightened, looking at her with a sad smile, still holding *The Book of Gems*.

"It's beautiful, isn't it?"

"It's a fake gem," she said to Xachar. "It's worse than that. It's—"

Xachar moved closer. "That's not something you should say. It's beautiful."

The press had stopped creating anything but more of itself—of the emerald. And yet Xachar couldn't see how monstrous it was.

She looked at the boy's eyes. They were ink-filled. So were his fingernails. He had a small crust of green glass at one wrist. "Xachar, you are in deep danger."

But Xachar shook his head. "I'm filled with knowledge. I can show you." He reached for Jorit.

Ania cried out and put two of the blank books on the press. As they slid through the mechanism, the emerald paled, trying to pull ink from empty pages.

Xachar groaned and swung his hand to knock the books from the rollers. They clattered to the floor, splayed and torn.

Xachar reached for Ania. And the clock began to tick faster.

"No!" Ania cried. "Wait. We can't leave now."

Jorit lurched forward—Ania couldn't leave. *Not this now. This here.*

But it was too late, the clock glowed, and she could feel the heat. And Jorit was falling toward the press, away from Ania. Jorit put her hand out for balance on the press, and the emerald spread quickly, covering her fingers, trapping her.

Calm, stay calm. She tried to tug her hand away. The emerald groaned. Xachar turned from Ania to grab Jorit's hand and hold it still.

With her other hand, Jorit grasped Ania's shoulder. "Go," she said. "Hurry. There's still time to get this right. They are trying to use the press to change everything." She could keep Ania from harm. She could help stop the press.

But Ania blinked, her eyes no longer brown and still filled with tears. Her opal-colored eyes gleamed as she whispered, "I know. They're trying to rewrite the past."

"You attempted to poison the press!" Xachar countered, his voice breaking. "To hurt the emerald." In his anger, he pressed Jorit against the machine. The emerald grew faster, up Jorit's hand, facets tightening around her arm. As the gem grew, she felt things she knew—names, places—draining away.

The room wavered. The smell of ink overpowered her senses.

A woman with a fierce expression, her braid swinging free, stood before Jorit. She held a clock. Jorit felt a memory tug at her, then disappear.

The woman's eyes blazed. They were beautiful and terrifying. "Time won't let you rewrite the past,

Xachar," she said, sounding sad.

Then with a yell, the woman raised the clock over her head. An opal glowed, bound within the clock's bent gears.

The pale, ink-stained boy lunged away from where he'd gripped Jorit, toward the woman. He shouted, "No, I must keep it running!" but the woman brought the clock down hard on the press. The clock's frame splintered, but its brass gears and the opal they contained jammed into the dark gem, beside Jorit's trapped arm.

When the clock-bound gem smashed the press, it seemed to scream. The woman screamed with it. And when it screamed, all the ink flooded away, tagging everything in its path with traces.

On Jorit's face, a small swirl of ink curled. On the woman—Jorit knew her suddenly—Ania's arm, a swash. Xachar's eyes filled with the ink and then ran free, in dark tears.

"I didn't know," he whispered.

Cracks ran along the emerald with a sound like ice breaking in a Far Reaches harbor.

When a crack spread the length of two facets, more breaks spawned from it, until the fake gem collapsed into dust.

Jorit shook her arms free. She reached for Ania, overwhelmed as all of the memories of their travels flooded back. She knew now what she hadn't wanted to admit before, in the crush of stopping the press. She didn't want this person to disappear again.

Ania held her hand tightly.

A loud, creaking groan filled the room.

Without the gem to hold it up, the press listed sideways. Its stressed mechanisms began to disassemble and crack. Pieces fell from it; gears and shafts and rollers struck the floor. When the ink scupper fell away, a cloud of dust rose into the air. As Jorit and Ania held their breath, the dust shaped words that had been stripped from the world in the name of knowledge.

Compendiums of Knowledge stored in the room began to leak. Dark ribbons of ink seeped onto floors and walls.

The ink formed stolen letters, crawling across the floor into words, each one writing itself back, moving fast across the room, under the door, out the windows, in search of their own books, signs, and papers.

Rubbing her arm, Jorit stepped from the room, Ania supporting her. They clutched several books they'd managed to save from the press.

Xachar sped past them into the barracks. Jorit let him go. The ink had left his eyes. Soon he knelt next to a woman who was slowly blinking, the light coming back to her own eyes. "Aunt," Jorit heard Xachar murmur, "where are the others?"

All around Jorit and Ania, waves of ink swept over the ground and through the air. They followed lines of ink out of the barracks, into East Quadril. Others walked with them, Pressmen and townspeople both, all staring as the ink flowed into words, seeking out the books and shelves where they'd been before.

They passed the library in Quadril, which had been sunk into its foundations. There, words paved the streets outside and decorated the buildings nearby. The blank books Jorit had rescued from the pressroom were soon filled with letters again.

Ania held the former clock's pieces together in her hands, unconsciously clicking her tongue against the roof of her mouth as she walked until Jorit steadied her.

The librarian lifted her eyes, opal-colored now, and stared at the town, the books in her hands. "Yes, I agree."

She turned and kissed Jorit's cheek quickly, almost bashfully. "You didn't have to stay," the librarian said.

"Yes I did," Jorit replied, pulling Ania to a stop in front of the library. "I wanted to see what would happen next."

"We happened next," the librarian whispered. "We

changed the future. I can see it."

Jorit felt the librarian's skin pressed against hers, the glow of her opal eyes and the steam from the pressroom drawing sweat across her palms. She felt the pulse of her heart, like a clock speeding up, and felt her own heart keep time with it.

She ran her fingers across Ania's cheek. Soft as a moth. Kissed her lips, even softer.

After a moment, she whispered, "We happen next."

They clasped hands, the last gem-bearer and the thief. Around them, East Quadril erupted in shouts, the Pressmen's barracks emptied, and the world flooded with words once more.

Acknowledgments

Many thanks to Tor.com for giving the Gemworld its proper setting. To my editor, Patrick Nielsen Hayden, and to Irene Gallo, for their vision; to Lee Harris, Mordicai Knode, Tommy Arnold, Anita Okoye, Rachel Bass, Lauren Hougen, and Ana Deboo.

To Paul Race and to Chris Wagner, who let me mess about with metals, stones, and oxygen-acetylene torches. To my first library, Tredyffrin, and to many of my favorites, including the Peabody, Trinity, the Enoch Pratt, the Library of Congress, the Bodleian, Northwest Akron, the Alderman, the New York Public Library, and the Free Library of Philadelphia. To all the librarians and timekeepers in my life, friends, family, and those I've met in the stacks.

To E. Catherine Tobler, Kelly Lagor, Nicole Feldringer, Chris Gerwel, Lauren Teffeau, Aliette de Boddard, Ryan Labay, Lynne M. Thomas, Siobhan Carroll, A. T. Greenblatt, Sarah Pinsker, A. C. Wise, and my agent, Barry Goldblatt, who were all very patient with facets of this story.

To everyone who loves books, or time, or who knows that a little bit of time travel happens whenever a page (or a phrase) is well turned, this is for you.

About the Author

Photograph by Dan Magus

FRAN WILDE's novels and short stories have been finalists for three Nebula Awards, two Hugo Awards, and a World Fantasy Award. They include her Andre Norton– and Compton Crook–winning debut novel, *Updraft*; its sequels, *Cloudbound* and *Horizon*; the middle-grade novel *Riverland*; and the novelette "The Jewel and Her Lapidary." Her short fiction has appeared in *Asimov's, Tor.com, Beneath Ceaseless Skies, Uncanny, Shimmer, Nature,* and the 2017 *Year's Best Dark Fantasy and Horror* anthology. She lives in Philadelphia with her family.

TOR · COM

Science fiction. Fantasy. The universe. And related subjects.

*

More than just a publisher's website, *Tor.com* is a venue for **original fiction, comics,** and **discussion** of the entire field of SF and fantasy, in all media and from all sources. Visit our site today—and join the conversation yourself.